#6

Stanley Cup Dream

THE MITCHELL BROTHERS SERIES

#6
Stanley Cup Dream

THE MITCHELL BROTHERS SERIES

Brian
McFarlane

Fenn Publishing Company Ltd.
Bolton, Canada

STANLEY CUP DREAM
BOOK SIX IN THE MITCHELL BROTHERS SERIES
A Fenn Publishing Book / September 2004

Copyright 2004 © Brian McFarlane

No part of this book may be reproduced or transmitted in any form, or
by any means, electronic or mechanical, including photocopying,
recording, or by any information storage and retrieval system, without
the written permission of the publisher.

The content, opinion and subject matter contained herein is the written expression of the author and does not reflect the opinion or ideol-
ogy of the publisher, or that of the publisher's representatives.

Fenn Publishing Company Ltd.
Bolton, Ontario, Canada

Distributed in Canada by H. B. Fenn and Company Ltd.
Bolton, Ontario, Canada, L7E 1W2
www.hbfenn.com
Library and Archives Canada Cataloguing in Publication

McFarlane, Brian, 1931-
        Stanley Cup dream / Brian McFarlane.

(Mitchell Brothers series ; 6)
For ages 8–12.
ISBN 1-55168-259-1

        1. Stanley Cup (Hockey)—History—Juvenile fiction.
2. Hockey—History—Juvenile fiction. I. Title. II. Series: McFarlane,
Brian, 1931- Mitchell Brothers series ; 6.

PS8575.F37S73 2004   jC813'.54   C2004-904390-0

STANLEY CUP DREAM

NOTE FROM THE AUTHOR

Almost every young person who plays hockey has dreamed of playing for the Stanley Cup. Only a select few ever get to realize that dream.

Back in 1936, the Mitchell brothers, Max and Marty, had that common dream. To their amazement, a wise old Indian Chief, Chief Echo of the Tumbling Waters Reserve, helped them make their dream almost come true. With the aid of his friends, the Little People, Chief Echo arranged for Max and Marty to skate down the River of Time and meet One-Eyed Frank McGee, the fabulous Ottawa hockey star of a century ago, the Wayne Gretzky of his era.

It was an extraordinary adventure. Max and Marty quickly learned that a player's passion for hockey was as strong in that era as it is today, and the riveting battles they witnessed up close for the Stanley Cup were, as Max would later report, "awesome" and "spine-tingling."

Grab your skates and join the Mitchell brothers—on the River of Time.

Brian McFarlane

CHAPTER 1

STANLEY CUP LORE

"Did you know a hockey team once put two goalies in the net—at the same time?" Max Mitchell said to his brother Marty.

"Get out of here. Two goalies aren't allowed."

"They were in 1903. Says so right in this book." Max held up the book he was reading: *Tales of the Stanley Cup*.

"Okay, I'll bite. How come a team used two goalies?"

Marty put down his hot chocolate and his Hardy Boys book, *The Shore Road Mystery*, and moved around the kitchen table behind Max. He peered at the pages of the hockey book over his brother's shoulder.

"It says here," Max said, pointing at a page, "that in 1903, the coach of the Kenora Thistles decided to try two goalies one night. He took one of his forwards and played him in goal next to the regular goalie."

"Did the strategy work?"

"No. The two goalies stumbled into each other and fell down a lot. And when the puck went into their net, they blamed each other for the score. The coach never tried it again and the league brought in a new rule. From then on only one goalie could play."

"That a library book?" asked Marty.

"Yep. Just came in. There are some fascinating stories in here. In one early day Stanley Cup game the puck fell through a hole in the ice and was lost until spring when the ice melted. And in those days, the goal judge stood right out on the ice behind the net. If a goal was scored, he waved a hankie in the air. Can you imagine that happening today—in 1936?"

"Wow," Marty said, chuckling at the image. "No way. Is there another goalie story in there? That's my position."

"Here's another one. A goalie named Fred Chittick refused to play in a Stanley Cup game until the manager gave him a bunch of free tickets for the match."

"No kidding," Marty said.

"And in 1923, an Ottawa player named King Clancy became the only man in history to play every position in a Stanley Cup game."

"Wait a minute," Marty protested. "You mean every position but goalie."

"No, he played in goal, too. In those days, if a goalie was given a penalty, he had to go sit in the penalty box. Clancy had already played all three forward positions and both defence positions because his team was short of players. When Benedict, the Ottawa goalie, was penalized, he handed Clancy his goal stick. He told him, 'Clancy, take care of this net. I'll be back in a couple of minutes.'"

Marty laughed. "That's wild. Did the other team score on him?"

"The other team was Edmonton. No, they didn't score. So Clancy has a perfect record as a goaltender in Stanley Cup play."

Max began to chuckle. He was a muscular youth with ash blond hair and blue eyes. Almost six feet tall, he excelled in most sports. His brother Marty was shorter, stockier, and two years younger. Marty had a thatch of reddish-brown hair and was known for his lively sense of humour.

"What's so funny?" asked Marty.

"It says here Clancy took the Stanley Cup home to Ottawa that summer and left it in his parlour. When friends came in they filled it with cigar and cigarette butts. It was used as an ashtray!"

"Well, that's better than using it as a chamber pot. Or to wash your socks in."

"Or a cuspidor," added Max, "you know, guys spit tobacco juice in them. You see it in the movies."

Both boys laughed some more.

Like his brother, 15-year-old Marty had a keen

3

interest in hockey. He said, "How about letting me read that book when you're finished?"

"Sure," said Max. "Hey, here's a good one. It's about the Montreal team that won the Stanley Cup in 1924. They left it on a street corner when they were en route to a victory party."

"Honest!" exclaimed Marty. "How come?"

"Flat tire," shrugged Max. "When they changed the tire they set the Cup on the curb. They forgot about it when they drove off. You can bet the owner of the team was really upset when his players showed up without it. He made them race all the way back and pick it up."

"They were lucky it was still there. Some kids could have stolen it and pawned it."

"Is that what you would have done?" asked Max, looking up and grinning.

"Hmm," Marty hesitated. "Tough question. Especially if you believe in finders keepers. How much was the Stanley Cup worth in those days?"

"I dunno," Max said. "Lord Stanley paid about fifty bucks for it in 1893. By 1924 it must have been worth double that amount. At least. But I'm just guessing."

"I would have brought it back," Marty decided. "What would hockey be without the Stanley Cup?"

Max said, "Good question. Hey, Marty, here's something really interesting. Guess which team travelled the longest distance to play for the Cup, only to lose by the biggest score?"

"I haven't a clue."

"Then I'll give you a clue. There's lots of ice where they came from."

"Iceland?"

Max snorted. "Good guess, but no. Listen to this. In December, 1904, a team from Dawson City in the Yukon travelled over four thousand miles to play in a Stanley Cup series against Ottawa. It took almost a month for them to get to Ottawa, so it was early in 1905 before they even got to play."

"Really?" Marty said. "I didn't know that. Where's Dawson City anyway? Where's the Yukon?"

"North of British Columbia. It borders Alaska."

"They had a hockey team way up there? In 1904?"

"Sure did. And an indoor arena too. Built by men who discovered a lot of gold around Dawson City." Max found his place in the book.

"In those days there wasn't an NHL, so any town or city could challenge for the Stanley Cup. Only a couple of thousand people lived in Kenora, Ontario, so it was the smallest town to ever bid for the Cup. They won it, too, in 1907."

"Dad told me once the NHL started in 1917. So the NHL is what? About twenty years old?"

"Right. Anyway, Dawson City challenged the Ottawa team and the challenge was accepted. It says here some of the Ottawa players never dreamed that Dawson City would show up for the games."

"Why not?"

"Because it was an impossible journey. They had to leave Dawson City a month before the series began—in the dead of winter. They had to travel by bicycle, dogsled, steamship and train. And walking, of course."

"Walking?"

"Yes, walking. It was over three hundred miles from Dawson City to Whitehorse, the nearest big town where they went to catch a train. When their bicycles broke down in the snow, they walked most of the way to Whitehorse. Took them nine days to get there."

"Then what did they do?" Marty asked.

"They took the train to Skagway, on the coast of Alaska. Then they sailed on a tramp steamer to Seattle—that's in Washington State—and rode the train up to Vancouver. Finally, they boarded another train that took them across Canada to Ottawa."

"Who won the series, Dawson City or Ottawa?" Marty asked.

Before Max could answer, there was a knock on the kitchen door. "Anybody home?" a voice called out as the door swung open.

"Hey! Look who's here!" exclaimed Marty.

CHAPTER 2

SAMMY COMES CALLING

"It's Sammy Fox, the famous lacrosse and hockey player," Marty said teasingly as he got up to greet their friend from Tumbling Waters, the nearby Indian reserve. "Come on in, Sammy. Take off your coat. Want some hot chocolate? Want to hear a joke?"

"Sure. Joke first, then the hot chocolate."

Marty said, "The doctor tells his patient he has only three weeks to live. So the patient says, 'Okay, Doc. I'll take the last two weeks in August and the week before Christmas.' " Marty giggled and slapped his thigh. "Get it?"

Sammy groaned and made a face.

"Hi, Sammy," Max said, rolling his eyes at Marty and getting up to pour their friend a hot chocolate. He pushed the cookie jar in front of Sammy. "What brings you to town?"

"Oh, the girls in high school drew up a petition.

They're demanding that I show up more often and give them more of my time. All the girls signed it." He shrugged. "So here I am."

"Sure, Sammy," Marty scoffed. "The way I hear it, your name was second on that list—right behind mine."

"You're quick, Marty," Sammy laughed. "Except maybe in goal." He reached for a cookie and looked around. "Where's your big husky—Big Fella?"

"We had to let him out to do his doggie business," Max explained, fanning the air with one hand. "He was farting something awful."

"You sure it was Big Fella?" Sammy asked innocently. He and Max looked at Marty.

"Come on, fellows," grumbled Marty. "Knock it off."

Sammy reached over and punched Marty lightly on the shoulder. "Just kidding, Marty." He said to Max, "Max, remember what you said the other day about the Little People?" He popped another cookie in his mouth. "Mmm. Chocolate chip. My favourite," he mumbled. "Your mom makes great cookies. She's not home?"

"She's down at the newspaper office, helping Dad get the *Review* out," said Marty.

"Sure, I remember," Max said. "When Marty and I spent time on your reserve a few weeks ago, we learned all about the Little People. Chief Echo told us about them. He said that long ago, a young hunter came upon a great ravine, climbed down to the bottom, and found himself hundreds of feet below sea level. There he met a magical tribe, the tiniest men and women the young man had ever seen."

"Right. The hunter gave them a pheasant he'd shot with his bow and arrow," Sammy nodded. "So they invited him to dinner. According to the legends of our people, the Little People control all the forces of nature. They shake the trees and the flowers in the spring to wake them up after the long sleep in winter. Then the Little People put them to sleep again in the fall."

Max was about to speak but his brother waved him off.

"Wait!" Marty cried out excitedly, remembering Chief Echo's story. "Didn't one of the Little People pick up a big stone and hurl it at a tree? To show the hunter that Little People were very strong? The stone hit the tree with such force that it split in two and caught on fire. Then they fed the young man from a bowl that never emptied and a cup that was always full. I remember that!"

Sammy Fox, whose tribal name was Sammy Running Fox, laughed. "You have a good memory, Marty."

"What are you getting at, Sammy?" Marty asked, his curiosity piqued.

"Remember the powwow we held when you were with us?" Sammy asked. "How we felt the strange presence of the Little People among us?"

"Sure," said Max. "You said they flew to the village and danced at the powwow but we were never able to see them because they are too shy to reveal themselves."

"We left some food for them on a nearby rock," added Marty. "But when we looked for it later, it had disappeared. That was amazing!"

Sammy turned serious. "So you believe in them, Max?"

Max frowned. "I'm not sure," he confided. "I could feel a . . . presence . . . that night at the powwow. I'll never forget it." He looked at Sammy. "Why do you ask?"

Sammy reached for another cookie, and then chewed thoughtfully.

"It's because of what you said the other day," Sammy resumed. "About how you'd like to go back in time and visit with hockey players of long ago. And one in particular."

"Back in time!" barked Marty. "How? Are you serious?"

"Sammy," said Max, "what's going on?"

Sammy smiled. "What's happened, Max, is this: Chief Echo wants to see you. He appreciates everything you did for our people when you were living among us. He'd like to make your dream come true."

Max gasped. "My dream? You mean my dream of meeting One-Eyed Frank McGee? The famous hockey star with the Ottawa Silver Seven? The greatest player of his day?"

Sammy nodded.

Max was incredulous. "But Sammy, One-Eyed Frank played hockey more than thirty years ago!"

Sammy smiled, and shrugged, as if travelling back in time was as simple as walking to the local hockey rink.

"Let's go see Chief Echo. He will show you how you can travel down the River of Time, going back dozens of years. For a brief time, you can live in the home of Frank McGee. You can watch him play for the Stanley Cup against Dawson City. You can meet his teammates and his opponents. You can decide if he really deserves to be one of your hockey idols."

"This is incredible. Will I be able to talk to him?" Max asked. "Better still, will I be able to play hockey with him, like in a team scrimmage, maybe?"

"Sure. You'll be his new friend. Just tell him you've come to Ottawa from the North Country. You're visiting for a while."

Max beamed, his eyes wide as saucers. Then he looked panicked. He ran a hand through his unruly blond hair. "Should I get a hair cut? How will I dress for this trip? How long will I be gone? Four weeks? Six?"

Sammy roared with laughter. "No, no, no. The Chief will put you gently to sleep, that's all. It's like hypnosis but you won't be asked to do stupid things like wear your shoes on your hands or imitate a jackass. It'll be very relaxing, you'll see. The Chief and the Little People will send you on a trip that might seem like six weeks, or six years. But you will be asleep for only a few minutes. Half an hour, maybe. Don't worry about bringing clothes or even skates. It will all work out when you get there."

Marty was bursting. "Can I go, too, Sammy? I want to go on a trip with Max!"

Sammy looked at Max. "That's entirely up to Max. You can bring Marty along if you like."

Max looked at his brother. Marty was two years younger but they got along well for the most part. Max hesitated. Then he said, "I'd be glad to take a kid brother along, if he showed me he really appreciated it. Like by treating me to an ice cream sundae . . ."

Marty shoved a hand in his pocket. He held up two shiny quarters. "Got fifty cents, enough for two ice cream sundaes. Does that mean I'm in?"

"Yep. You're in," Max said with a grin. "Just don't embarrass me when we get to Ottawa by telling some of your silly jokes. And the sundaes you're buying can wait till we get back."

"Let's go. Let's go!" Marty cried. "By the way, Sammy. Have you ever been down the River of Time? Why don't you come with us?"

Sammy nodded. "No, thanks. Not this time. And yes, I've had a couple of trips down the River of Time. Two incredible journeys I'll never forget. I only go when Chief Echo invites me to. You must be a very special person in his eyes to receive an invitation. And besides . . ."

"Besides what, Sammy?" asked Marty.

Sammy sighed. "Besides, those high school girls made me promise I'd stay close. Think of all the broken hearts if I left."

Max burst our laughing while Marty said, "You poor guy. I know exactly how you feel."

"You do?" Sammy asked.

"Sure. Nobody's a bigger teen idol in this town than I am." Marty began throwing on his jacket. "Ready?" he asked. "Let's go then. It'll be good to see Chief Echo again. Hey, Sammy, I just thought of something. The Chief may have enough magic powers to send us on a trip down the River of Time, but . . ."

"But what, Marty?"

"But will he have enough magic gas left to get us back again?"

Max and Sammy laughed. Sammy said, "I'm sure he will. If not, we'll send the Little People after you. They can always fly you back."

CHAPTER 3

SKATING ON THE
RIVER OF TIME

Sitting cross-legged in his longhouse on the Tumbling Waters Indian Reserve, Chief Echo folded his arms across his broad chest and closed his eyes. Max and Marty could see his lips moving but they could hear no words, no sound at all. Earlier, Chief Echo had motioned the Mitchell brothers to sit on hand-woven Indian mats placed in front of him. The crackling fire warmed his longhouse, and smoke drifted in lazy banners up through a hole in the sloping roof.

Now the Chief cupped his ear with one hand. He appeared to be listening to something—or some-one—listening intently—but the only sounds in the longhouse came from the nearby fire.

After a few minutes he opened his eyes, relaxed, and smiled. "That was the Chief of the Little People speaking to me. He was here in my longhouse. Of course, I could not see him."

The Chief took a long stick at his side and poked at the coals in the fire.

"The Chief of the Little People suggested I take you boys to a small longhouse on the very edge of the reserve," he continued. "It is quiet there, isolated. There is nothing to fear. There the Little People will surround you. They will cover you with magic blankets. Blankets you can neither see nor feel. They will dance over your heads and laugh and sing. The joy and happiness and high spirits they feel will be uplifting. These feelings will rub off on you. You will be relaxed and happy. Within moments, you will enter a deep sleep. While asleep, you will share the same dream, a remarkable dream. It will mark the start of your journey."

Marty looked puzzled and raised one hand, as if he were in a classroom. "Chief Echo, did you say we'd share the same dream? I've never heard of two people sharing a dream."

Chief Echo rose to his feet and smiled. "There are many mysteries in life, Marty. The Little People will treat you to a journey down the River of Time. And when the riverbanks merge—even momentarily—you will know that you have reached your destination."

"Wow!" said Marty. "I'm so excited I can't wait. But I'm sure I won't be able to sleep. Not with Little People dancing over my head."

Chief Echo chuckled. "Oh, you will sleep, all right. The invisible blankets will see to that. You see, if you believe in the Little People, anything is possible. Come, let us walk to the small longhouse. Your adventure is about to begin."

Max and Marty found themselves sitting on a snowbank, donning their skates. They were on the banks of a massive frozen river—the River of Time. The sparkling surface stretched ahead of them as far as their eyes could see.

"I've never seen the sky so blue or the ice so hard and smooth," Max said.

"Or the air so fresh," echoed Marty, sniffing. "Smells a lot sweeter than our hockey dressing room."

"I feel so . . . so energized," said Max.

"I can't remember when I've ever felt better," Marty agreed.

The river ice was a shimmering glacial blue. Oddly, there was not a flake of snow on the surface, although the banks were thick with it.

"Looks like we won't have far to skate," Marty observed, screening his eyes with one hand. "You can see where the riverbanks merge already."

Max chuckled. "Marty, when we skate down the river, the banks will stay as far apart as they are right here. Your eyes deceive you if they tell you that they merge at the horizon."

"I get it," Marty said sheepishly. "I should have known that. It's like an optical delusion."

"Illusion," Max corrected. "Optical illusion."

"That's what I just said," Marty argued.

"Come on, let's go, brother," Max said, pulling Marty to his feet. "This could be one of the best adventures of our lives."

They skated out on the ice, tentatively at first.

"This is the best ice I've ever skated on," Marty said. "Not a bump, not a crack. It's unbelievable." With a whoop of joy, he sprinted ahead and Max followed.

"Ice so thick there's not a chance we'll fall through it," Max said. He took long, graceful strides and flew effortlessly over the slick surface, Marty close at his side.

"Look, Max! The trees and hills we're passing are just a blur," Marty shouted. "We must be skating a hundred miles an hour!"

Max glanced toward the riverbank. To his surprise, hundreds of people were gathered there. All of the faces were familiar.

"Marty, there's Mom and Dad and Uncle Jake! There's our friend Trudy Reeves. And Big Fella is barking and wagging his tail. All the people in Indian River are waving to us and cheering us on."

The boys flew down the ice.

"They're gone, Max," said Marty, surprised. "Gone in a second. I waved back but they're already out of sight. What's that up ahead?"

"It's a huge black cloud. Look! Under the cloud there's a crowd of people." Max noticed, as they approached, that the people were dressed in ragged clothes and they looked terribly dejected. "I know who they are," said Max. "They're Depression people. Broke and cold and hungry." Some of the people were standing in long lines, waiting for a piece of bread or a bowl of soup. One of them was holding out a sign on which he had written: Brother, Can You Spare a Dime?

"They're gone, too, Max," said Marty. "Behind us now. Look! The sun is out and more people are on the shore. Happy people. There's singing and dancing to happy music."

"They're dancing the Charleston, Marty. A crazy dance from the 1920s. Look over there!" In the distance Max and Marty saw ballparks and football fields. Boxing rings and golf courses! There was Babe Ruth hitting a home run! And Jack Dempsey, the heavyweight boxing champ. "It's the Golden Age of Sports!" Max shouted breathlessly.

"Let's stop, Max," begged Marty. "I can get Babe Ruth's autograph."

"We can't stop, Marty. Remember what the Chief said. If we stop before we reach our chosen destination, the Little People will call us back. I want to reach Ottawa. I want to meet One-Eyed Frank McGee."

They skated on, gliding across the ice at breath-taking speed.

"Oh, oh," Marty said. "Another huge black cloud just ahead. And the sound of gun fire." They heard rifles, machine guns, and huge cannons. And the rumbling of tanks and the buzzing roar of planes in murderous dog fights. "Looks like a big war to me," said Marty.

"It was a big war, Marty," agreed Max. "The Great War. It lasted from 1914 to 1918. Uncle Jake was in it. He was lucky to survive. It was a terrible war."

"Max, you were right about the shore lines. They look like they're coming together up ahead but we've skated miles and they're still far apart."

"The Little People said they would meet; and they will, when we reach our destination. Have faith, Marty. Be a believer."

The boys noticed there were fewer and fewer cars on the roads. Horse-drawn carts and sleighs had replaced them. Men were busy laying down railroad track. Pioneers in wagons were heading west to places like California and the vast Canadian prairies.

"We're getting closer," shouted Max. "You tired yet?"

"No, that's the funny part. I've never skated so far and so fast and yet been so full of energy. I'm really excited about getting to Ottawa and making friends with Frank McGee."

In the distance, high on a hill, Max noticed a huge building on a high cliff overlooking the river. Other buildings nearby were almost as big. He nudged Marty and pointed.

"Marty, we're almost there. Those are Canada's Parliament buildings. Where the prime minister leads his party in debates against the opposition. And there's the famous Rideau Canal cutting through the centre of the city. Look at all the kids playing hockey and skating on the canal! Look at all the horse-drawn sleds charging in all directions."

"How old is Canada's capital city?" Marty asked.

Without knowing how the information came to him, Max was able to answer.

"The city was founded in 1827 by Colonel John By, who supervised the construction of the Rideau Canal. At first it was called Bytown. But long before that, in 1800, Philemon Wright, an American from Massachusetts, marched five hundred miles through deep snow to come here and begin a settlement at nearby Chaudière Falls. He brought his wife, six children, five other families and a dozen other folks to homestead here."

"When did it get to be the Capital City?" Marty asked.

"In 1857. A lot of cities—Quebec City, Montreal, Kingston, Ottawa and Toronto—argued over which should be number one. Queen Victoria got to choose and she picked Ottawa."

Marty, who'd been half listening, let out a whoop. "Look, Max! The shores of the river have finally converged," he shouted. "That's our signal to get to shore. Our long skate is almost over. Man, that was great! But how are we ever going to find Frank McGee in a city so big? Look at all the houses and buildings. Must be ten thousand people living here."

"More like eighty or a hundred thousand," Max said. "Don't worry. The Little People will find a way to put us together. You'll see."

CHAPTER 4
MEETING FRANK MCGEE

Max and Marty Mitchell skated to shore, where they pulled off their skates in the shadow of the Parliament buildings. They donned warm winter boots plucked from bags they'd slung over their shoulders.

"Let's sit on that park bench and get accustomed to the sights of Ottawa," Max suggested.

From the bench, they marvelled at the hubbub in the town centre. Horse-drawn sleighs and cutters darting in all directions, children tobogganing on a nearby hill, snowshoers tramping through the park, a steady stream of people moving in and out of the Parliament buildings. A streetcar, its bell clanging, came into view, following tracks that ran down Sparks Street and on toward Bank Street. Max and Marty waved to the people inside.

Suddenly, one of the single horse sleighs veered off the street. Its driver steered it toward the boys.

The horse wore a silver harness. Bells attached to it jingled merrily as the sleigh crunched over the hard-packed snow. The horse was breathing heavily and appeared to be happy to stop on the command of the driver. "Whoa, Cinderella, Whoa!"

"Hey, you boys!" a voice called out. "Are you the Mitchells?"

For a long moment, Max and Marty could only stare, speechless, at the two men in the sleigh. The man who called out was a handsome man, despite the fact that he wore a black patch over his right eye. His face was ruddy from the cold. His left eye, blue as a summer sky, sparkled and his blond hair fell over his face when a gust of winter wind flew across the sleigh.

The man next to him was obviously a brother or a cousin. He had the same facial characteristics, the same sturdy build, the same thick hair. He looked older and perhaps a bit less fun-loving than his companion.

Finally Max stammered, "We're the Mitchells. How come you know us?"

"I'm Frank McGee!" the eye-patch man crowed. "This is my brother Jim. We're on our way to Dey's Arena. I heard you were coming to town. Want a lift?"

"We'd love one, Mr. McGee," Max said, jumping to his feet. "We came all the way from the North Country just to meet you."

"Our Dad runs a newspaper there—in Indian River," Marty added. "My brother would like to write an article about you for the paper. He's a good writer."

"Fine with me," McGee exclaimed. "Come on, get in! Bring your skates. There's a buffalo-fur robe in back. Put it around your feet and over your knees. And call me Frank or Frankie. Everybody does. We'll talk more after hockey practice."

Within minutes, the sleigh delivered them to Dey's Arena on Gladstone Avenue, home of the famous Ottawa Silver Seven hockey club, the world champions and Stanley Cup holders. It was the largest arena the Mitchell boys had ever seen. There was seating for almost five thousand fans. McGee and his brother rushed down a corridor toward the dressing room.

"Have to hurry. We're almost late," McGee explained. "Coach will fine us fifty cents if we're late. Find a seat and enjoy the practice."

Max and Marty took rinkside seats and waited for McGee and his mates on the Silver Seven to appear. There were a number of spectators—perhaps a dozen or two.

"Newspapermen mostly," guessed Marty. "They're carrying pads and pencils. Hear them speaking French? Some must be from Montreal. They're here for the big game tomorrow night."

Max and Marty looked all around, noting the freshly painted white boards, the scoreboard at one end under a big clock, the glistening natural ice surface where many of the world's greatest players displayed their skills on skates.

Max was awestruck. "Lord Stanley, the Governor General, donated the Stanley Cup to hockey in 1893," he said. "Many of the big battles for the Cup have been decided right here."

"Look at the crude goal nets, Max!" Marty said, pointing. "They're really primitive. And there's no goal line painted on the ice connecting the two posts."

"That's true, Marty. But remember it's only 1905. Until a couple of years ago there were no nets at all. Just a couple of sticks stuck in the ice. The introduction of nets—crude as they may be—has eliminated a lot of arguments over whether a goal should count or not."

The Ottawa players, led by goalie Bouse Hutton, came onto the ice and skated around in lazy circles, warming up, getting loose. Max and Marty, both star players back home on the Indian River junior club, watched Hutton closely.

Marty, a goalie, whispered to Max, "Look at him. No special skates, the flimsiest pads I've ever seen, and gloves so small and thin it's a wonder all his fingers aren't broken. And his goal stick is so . . . so . . . battered."

"Pretty poor protection, isn't it?" Max agreed. "All he's got to protect his privates is a thick glove shoved down his pants."

Marty groaned at the thought and shifted in his seat. "Looks like he's used that old goal stick in every game for the past four or five years," he said. "It's ready for the scrap heap."

"Here comes McGee," Max interrupted.

The Ottawa star glided onto the ice to polite applause and moments later circled the rink at top speed.

"What a skater! He's a real smoothie," Marty said, standing to get a better look.

"You'd think he was born with skates on," Max said. "He glides around the ice like a phantom."

Two middle-aged men entered the arena and stood by the low boards, just a few feet away from the Mitchells. One of them sported a red plaid jacket, the other a heavy fur coat. Max and Marty could hear them talking about hockey generally and the Silver Seven in particular. It wasn't long before one of them mentioned Frank McGee.

"I've seen all the greats of the game," said Mr. Plaid Jacket. "Most of them have played here in Ottawa at one time or another. But Frankie is always the best man on the ice. A hockey wonder he is. Look at him! He only weighs about 140 pounds. Hi, Frankie," the man called out as McGee sped by. He was rewarded with a brief smile and a nod from McGee as he skated on.

Plaid Jacket grabbed Fur Coat conspiratorially by the arm. "When I first saw him a few years ago, I thought he was soft, too soft and delicate, likely to quit if he got a good slap with a stick." He shook his head at the recollection. "He was far different than the man I envisioned after reading his press clippings, I expected to see a lumbering brute, a hulking savage. I sure was fooled. When he stepped on the ice he was a regular dude. His golden hair was parted precisely in the centre. His hockey pants were snow white and someone—his mother perhaps—had pressed them so they showed a sharp crease."

"His looks surprised you?" Fur Coat asked.

Plaid Jacket threw his head back and roared, "Why, I was stunned! I asked his coach if that really was One-Eyed Frank McGee. He smiled cagily at me, and merely nodded. The Ottawas played Winnipeg that night and I'll never forget the tremendous roar that went up when McGee glided out on the ice. The fans bellowed 'McGee! McGee! McGee!' It was so loud that some people covered their ears."

He sketched the scene with his hands, reminiscing. "In the warm-up, he handled his stick as easily as he would a knife and fork. When the game began, I never saw speed or stickhandling like it. He could skate like a ghost, even though he was closely checked by two determined young men on the Winnipegs."

"But was the lad as good in games away from home?" Fur Coat asked. "Sometimes there's a huge difference in a player's attitude and performance when he's at work in an unfriendly rink."

Plaid Jacket snorted derisively, dismissing the suggestion. "It didn't matter where he played! He would have been a marvel in Timbuktu. I saw him in Montreal several times, with about six thousand fans howling for his scalp. He was knocked out cold half a dozen times. But he survived to score the final two goals that won the contest. No one could slow him down or show him up. No one could stop him. What a silence fell over the arena when he scored that final goal with a minute to play." He paused in watchful silence as McGee skimmed a perfect pass to a teammate.

"Way to go, Frankie!" he brayed. "My, but he was game," he resumed, remembering McGee's heroics from a past performance, "taking the puck and beginning a series of slashing attacks while his opponents tried to eat him alive." Plaid Jacket described how McGee had barged through a forest of swinging sticks and battled his way right into the Montreal net. The goal judge had waved his flag while shaking his head in disbelief. McGee had skated off, flashing the same little smile he had started with.

"A smile like the one we just saw."

McGee sparkled during the practice session. The Silver Seven players whooped and hollered as they sprinted through some drills, then Petey Green, the coach, divided his squad in two for a brief scrimmage.

"Big game tomorrow night," Green told them. "Punch Pounder is in town with the Montreal Wanderers. I guess you all remember Punch and the dirty stuff he pulled last time we met."

Team captain Harvey Pulford snorted. "He gave me the butt end of his stick and cracked two of my ribs," he snarled.

Frank McGee said, "The so and so cracked me over the head with his stick until it broke."

"The stick or your head, Frankie?" asked a teammate innocently.

"The stick, you ninny," McGee answered, slapping his teammate on the rump with his stick blade.

"Isn't Punch the guy who put your eye out a couple of years ago?" one of the rookies in the club asked. "I read about it in the papers. Pounder claimed it was an accident."

McGee's body stiffened. He bristled. "It was no accident," he growled. "I passed him for the scoring lead that night and Punch couldn't take it. When I went around him for my fifth goal of the game, he came after me and slashed me in the eye with his stick. Doctors told me I'd never play hockey again. Well, here I am . . ."

"I'll bet you can't wait to meet Punch again tomorrow night," predicted goalie Bouse Hutton with a wry laugh.

McGee smiled, then turned serious. "Hockey can be a rough game, men," he said. "And some mean-spirited men play it. Like Pounder." He looked at his teammates. "But I swear I would never deliberately seek revenge. I keep my stick down. I couldn't think of injuring another player the way Pounder injured me. That's not hockey. That's not what this grand game is all about."

CHAPTER 5
THE MEANEST OPPONENT

"Try to stay away from Punch Pounder tomorrow night!" Coach Green told his assembled players. The Silver Seven were grouped around him at centre ice. "He's the meanest, dirtiest, rottenest player I've ever seen. I don't want him maiming one of you like he did Frankie. So stay away. And never turn your back on him."

He turned to McGee. "Punch will be out to get you, Frankie. We all know that. He's jealous of you and furious because you always show him up. Watch out for him."

"I will, Coach. I turned my back on him once. It cost me an eye. I'll never make that mistake again."

When the practice was over, Frank McGee skated over to the boards. "You fellows want to put on some gear? Marty, I understand you're a goalie."

"How'd you know that?" Marty asked, surprised.

"Never mind. Go in the dressing room. I see you

have your skates with you. The trainer will give you sticks and equipment. Some of the guys are going to play a little game of shinny."

"We'd love to!" Max and Marty blurted in unison. "Lucky for us we brought our skates."

Warming up a few minutes later, Marty told Frank he and Max had some questions.

"Fire away," said Frank.

"Why is your team called the Silver Seven?" asked Marty. "Aren't there any teams around named the Leafs or the Habs or the Red Wings?"

"Strange names," McGee answered quizzically. "Never heard of any of them. As for the name Silver Seven, a couple of years ago our owner gave each of the seven players on our team little silver nuggets. He got them from the big silver strike in the North Country. So we became known as the Silver Seven. Some fans like the name Senators better."

"There are only seven players on the team? No subs?"

"We have a couple of subs. But they only get to play if one of us gets hurt. Most of us play the full sixty minutes of every game. If one of us has to go off to be stitched up, or if his skate breaks, the visiting team either drops a player to make things even or they let us use one of our subs."

"It must be hard to get subs if they never get to play," Max observed.

Frank laughed. "Not really. Subs on any team have to learn to be patient, to wait for a chance to play. It's not easy but there's also the honour that goes with being part of our team.

"On bitterly cold nights, the subs often stay in our dressing room, playing cards around the potbellied stove. They don't even get to see the game."

"The fans must suffer on those nights," said Max. "It's colder in here than in a polar bear's cave."

Frankie agreed. "Fans come from all over to see us play," he said. "They come in sleighs from all the small towns around. They bundle up in fur coats and plenty of blankets. They heat bricks and place them in the bottom of the sleigh. That keeps their feet warm—until the bricks cool off, that is.

"Last season a family of five got lost in a blizzard going home from a game. They were found the next day up the Ottawa River. All were gone, frozen to death in their sleigh."

McGee slapped his stick on the ice three times. "Come on, boys, let's have some fun. Let's play shinny."

Moments later, Max and Marty found themselves involved in a three on three game with several of the Stanley Cup champions.

Max was thrilled when Frank McGee said, "You play up front with me, Max. Harvey Pulford, our team captain, will play on defence." He turned to

Marty, who was wearing goaltending gear. "Marty, you play goal for the other team." He winked. "I want to see if you can stop a balloon."

"I'm not sure I can stop anything with these pads on," Marty said, smiling. "They're barely wide enough to cover my legs. And they're not much thicker than a doormat."

"Nonsense," snorted McGee. "They're top of the line. The club paid three dollars for them just last year. And that stick you've got is hand-made. Cost thirty-five cents."

Max wanted to ask McGee if the team had any longer sticks. He was tall and the Ottawa sticks were all too short for him. And the blades were too long. But he didn't dare complain. He noticed the other players were crouched over, using short sticks. Some of them—like Pulford—pushed the puck ahead using just one hand on his stick.

Once the game was underway Max quickly adjusted to McGee's smooth skating and stickhandling. Together they controlled the puck until McGee lashed a shot at Marty in the goal. Marty threw a glove out and made a brilliant save.

McGee brushed aside the save. "Beginner's luck," he joked. "Watch out for the next one."

He stepped up his pace and whistled three quick shots at Marty. Marty juggled the first one with his glove before trapping it. He stopped the other two with quick pad saves. On all three he moved out of his goal to face the shot, cutting down the angles.

McGee stopped by the net to praise him. "You're good, kid. Really good. Coming out of your net like that was risky. But smart. Truth is, I've never seen a goalie do that before."

"Thanks, Frankie," Marty said. "Coming from you, that's a great compliment."

Max drew similar praise from the Ottawa flash. "You can skate with anyone out here today, Max. And you can pass and stickhandle with the best of us. You boys really surprised me."

Max thought it must have something to do with the difference in eras. He was a modern player. Max believed that each generation produced better players than the ones preceding it. The lessons and tactics of one are passed on to the next. He said, "I'd be even better, Frank, if I could use a longer stick. Yours are only about three feet long."

McGee shrugged, confused. "They've always been this length, Max. What do you mean, a longer stick?"

Too late, Max realized his mistake. He was not in 1936. He was in an older era. "Uh, nothing. Never mind."

"I can't seem to score on your brother," Frank said, changing the subject. "Let's see if you can beat him."

Max took a pass from McGee and raced in on

Marty. At the last second, he pulled Marty to the right, and then shifted to the left, slipping the puck between his legs.

"Wow!" McGee said. "Some move."

"Marty and I call that a deke," Max said while Marty fished the puck out of the net. "I do that a lot back in Indian River."

"A deke, eh? Never heard that word before. Show me that move again, Max," McGee said. "I can use another trick like that one."

"I can show you another move my Uncle Jake taught me," Max said. He took the puck and moved in from the wing at a sharp angle. He faked a move in front of Marty who hugged the post. Then Max glided behind the net, came swiftly around the far post and tucked the puck in before Marty could move over to block.

"Nice going!" Frank shouted. "I'm going to practise that one, too. I'll call it Uncle Jake's move."

"Sure," said Max. "Although Uncle Jake calls it a wraparound."

After the scrimmage, Max and Marty mingled with the Silver Seven players in their dressing room. The men stripped off their jerseys and light padding and stood around in their soggy woollen underwear. Then they began donning their street clothes.

"Hey, Max," Marty whispered. "Where are the showers?"

"Not invented yet," Max whispered back. "The players probably go home and have a hot bath."

"Look! Their skate blades clamp right onto their boots. Never saw that before. And I can't believe they get by without a second and a third line."

"You heard what Frankie said, Marty. Most players never leave the ice. The seventh man is called a rover—an extra forward. If hockey ever has a Hall of Fame, some of these men will be in it."

Max and Marty heard laughter in the room. The players were passing around a copy of the Ottawa Journal.

"Look at this, boys," Frankie said. "Our boss has been speaking to the press again." He was referring to the president of their hockey club. "Seems Mr. Quinn wants to change the game and some of his proposals are hilarious. Take a look."

Max picked up the paper and read the article aloud.

President Quinn Wants to Change Hockey.
Suggests "Great New Rules"
For years hockey men have been arguing over the rules of the game. Should goal nets be allowed? Should teams carry six men or seven? Should goalies be allowed to flop to the ice? In an effort to reshape the game, the president of the Ottawa club, Mr. T. Emmett Quinn, has proposed the following rule changes:

1. To increase scoring opportunities, the puck should be painted green and reduced to half its present size, thus making it more difficult for goaltenders to see and to stop.

2. Players should be compelled to carry enough bills in their pockets to pay any fines they may receive on the spot.

3. Instead of giving a player a minor penalty, the referee should stop the play, take the offender to the side boards and have an earnest discussion with him for half a minute, so that he might reform him.

Mr. Quinn thought the proposed changes were good ones but his colleagues disagreed and voted them down unanimously.

"What do you think about those rules, Max?" Frankie asked.

"I've never seen a green puck," Max answered. "I take it Mr. Quinn is Irish? As for the referee taking a penalized player aside and trying to reform him, my guess is it wouldn't work with men like Punch Pounder. The ref might get a good punch in the nose for his trouble."

Marty raised his hand. "I think you should paint a line across the ice between the goal posts. It'll help settle a lot of disputes."

Max had another suggestion. "Maybe you should think about playing six-man hockey. You really don't need a rover out there. And you might want to put your names on your jerseys. Or numbers, so that fans can identify you on the ice."

"Hey, those are good ideas," Rat Westwick said, nodding his approval. "I've always thought the ice was too cluttered with seven players a side. And painting a goal line makes all kinds of sense."

The players murmured their approval.

"So do numbers on our sweaters," added Harvey Pulford. "We could even print the names and numbers of players on both teams on some paper. Call it a menu maybe. Or better still, a program. Hand them out before each game."

"Heck, we might even sell them," suggested Rat Westwick. "Add a place to keep score. Fans could keep the program as a souvenir. You could even put my picture on the cover. For a fee, of course."

"Your picture?" scoffed coach Petey Green. "Who wants a picture of a Rat? And it wouldn't be there because of your scoring prowess. You couldn't hit a hole in a ladder."

The Silver Seven looked at Max and Marty with new respect. Max wasn't just a flashy skater and Marty a precocious goalie Frank McGee had brought along to a practice. They were skilled and smart. They knew their hockey.

"Any other suggestions?" Frankie asked.

"I've got one," Marty said. "Back home, Max and his two wingers put little bells on their skates. That way they knew right where their linemates were on the ice."

"Hmm. Not a bad idea," said Rat. "I've got some cowbells at home."

"Forget about it, Rat," said Petey Green. "Cowbells! They'd drive everybody crazy. Too noisy and too heavy."

"Now we're going to lunch," Frank McGee stated. "And Bouse Hutton is paying."

"Why me, Frankie?" Hutton asked.

"Because the other night in Montreal, at the end of the game when the fans booed us and threw a lot of coins on the ice, you scooped them up. Then you borrowed a trash can from a rink attendant and pushed the coins under it."

"That's right," shouted a teammate. "Then you turned the can over and sat on it. The rest of us couldn't get at those coins. I figure you scooped up ten dollars—easy. So you can pay for lunch, Bouse."

Bouse Hutton laughed. "Okay, guys, I'll buy lunch. But some of those coins turned out to be worthless slugs. And a few were streetcar tokens. Still, I cleared more than six bucks. And that's after I tipped the guy who brought me the trashcan."

"That's more than enough for lunch," said Frankie.

Max and Marty laughed heartily. They had never heard of such a thing in hockey.

CHAPTER 6

THROUGH THE RIVER ICE

After the morning practice, Frank and Jim McGee gave the Mitchell brothers a tour of the city. The bells on the sleigh jingled as they swept along the city streets. Small boys often recognized the famous athlete and ran alongside, shouting, "Hi Frankie!" and "Have a good game tomorrow, Frankie" and "Hang one on Punch Pounder for me, Frankie."

The Mitchell brothers were given a brief tour of the Parliament buildings and the Royal Canadian Mint. Frank told them the history of the Rideau Canal and how its builder, Colonel By, a visionary, had insisted that it be made wide enough and long enough to accommodate huge boats. Boats yet to be built.

"It was good thinking," Frank said. "The original plans called for it to be a mere twenty feet wide. Hardly big enough to raise a canoe."

"Tell them about how the Stanley Cup wound up

in the canal," prompted Jim.

"Oh, that was the talk of the town," Frankie said, laughing. "After we won the Stanley Cup, we were walking from the arena to the Russell Hotel, to celebrate our victory.

"When we passed the canal, someone said to me, 'Frankie, you're a football player. Bet you can't drop kick the Cup into the canal!' Well, I was feeling pretty good, so without thinking much about it I kicked the Cup—rather gently I thought—but it soared high in the air and landed smack in the middle of the canal. None of us wanted to climb down there in the middle of the night. We might fall through the ice. But we hurried back the next morning. I climbed over the rail and dropped onto the canal. There was the Cup, half buried in snow. Not even a dent on it. It was just a foolish prank, one I'm embarrassed to talk about."

"But why?" asked Marty. "It's a funny story."

Frankie looked straight into Marty's eyes. "I don't think so, Marty," he said. "Not anymore. You see, the moment I kicked that Cup in the air I realized that I'd made a big mistake. Nobody should mistreat the Stanley Cup. Not me, not anybody. It's the symbol of what hockey's all about. It's a symbol of excellence."

Jim McGee chuckled. "When momma found out what Frankie had done, she made him run right off to church. Confess all to Father O'Malley."

Jim raised an arm and pointed across the broad expanse of the Ottawa River.

"Over there," he said, "across from the entrance to the canal, on the Quebec side, you can see the E. B. Eddy Match Company. A quarter of a century ago, in 1877, hundreds of women hand-dipped a million match heads a day. Boys, when you pick up a match you never think of how the head got there, do you?"

"We don't smoke, so we seldom use matches," Max said. "But a million a day. That's impressive."

They stopped for lunch at the famous Russell Hotel, where most of the visiting hockey teams stayed. Marty took one look at the menu and whistled quietly. "There's nothing on here for more than a dollar," he whispered to Max. "That's awfully cheap compared to Merry Mabel's place back home."

"Never mind the price, Marty. Everything seems really cheap in 1904. Order what you want. Frankie told me it's his treat."

"That's good," Marty chuckled. "I just might order two or three meals. Say, does Frankie get paid to play hockey?"

"No. All the Ottawa players are amateurs. But I suspect he may find a few dollars tucked inside his shoe when he gets dressed after a game."

Marty chuckled. "I guess somebody like the tooth fairy leaves the money there."

"Tooth fairy? What's a tooth fairy?" Frankie asked.

"Never mind. It was just a joke," Marty said.

"One of the visiting teams is here today," Jim McGee explained. "Some of the Montreal Wanderers are sitting at that long table in the corner."

One of them, a huge man, was involved in a heated discussion with a waiter. His booming voice thundered throughout the room.

"This soup is too hot," he howled. "I burned my mouth on it. I oughta pound you!"

"But, sir," the waiter replied meekly, "I warned you . . ."

"You did not!" roared the player. He lumbered to his feet, glowered menacingly, and then roughly flung the bowl of soup at the terrified waiter, soaking his uniform. The waiter fled to the kitchen.

"Punch Pounder," sighed Jim McGee, shaking his head. "He's got a wicked temper. What a menace!"

Pounder threw his napkin down and stomped toward the door. When he came upon the McGees, he stopped suddenly. "There you are, you little runt," he snarled. "The famous Frank McGee." He jabbed the air with a fat finger. "What a famous liar you are! Saying I knocked out your eye on purpose. You're nothing but a crybaby!"

He turned to the other diners in the room. "It ain't true, folks. It was an accident, honest. He's a rotten liar. Got me suspended. Almost ruined my career. Well, I'll fix him before I'm through."

McGee, fuming with suppressed rage, shot to his feet. He would have rushed Pounder if his brother Jim and Max hadn't restrained him. Frank's face was ruddy with fury and his fists were clenched.

"Accident!" he shouted. "Pounder, you told your teammates you were going to disable me. Then you bragged to them that you'd taken my eye out. One of them told me that. You deny it?"

"I do! I do deny it!" Pounder roared. "He's a liar, too. Like you."

Suddenly, four policemen rushed into the dining room and surrounded Pounder, who towered over them.

"Let's go, Pounder," a burly policeman said. "You've caused enough trouble for one day, fella." The policemen escorted him to the lobby and, after some discussion, allowed him to climb the stairs to his room. He shouted over his shoulder, "I'll get you, McGee! I'll fix it so you never play hockey again!"

The diners resumed eating and McGee, once again looking relaxed and composed, apologized to the Mitchells.

"Sorry about that," he said. "I wouldn't have come in here if I'd known the Wanderers were eating here. As for Punch Pounder . . . well, as you can see, he makes my blood boil."

"Aren't you afraid?" Marty asked Frank. "Afraid of

what Pounder might do to you tomorrow? Or in the game after that?"

"Not really," McGee said, smiling. "I've had tougher men than him come after me before. I'm used to it. I can take care of myself. It's just that none of the others left me with a lifelong souvenir, is all." He ruefully fingered his eye patch.

"Come on. Let's go home," Jim McGee said, getting to his feet. "We'll take the sleigh out on the river ice. It'll take us a bit longer to get home but the ride is worth it."

It was. Max and Marty enjoyed the dash over the snow-covered ice. They enjoyed the snort and stomp of the horse. They smiled when they heard the shouts and laughter of the young people around them, skaters and hockey players, whirling and dashing over a long sheet of ice they'd shovelled free of snow.

"Reminds me of us back in Indian River," Marty said.

Frank slowed the pace so Max and Marty could take in the sights.

"Hey, look!" Max shouted. "There's a girl playing hockey."

"That's Lady Marlene, the Governor General's daughter," Frankie said, waving in her direction. But she was too busy chasing a puck to see him.

"She's sixteen and a pretty good player," Jim said.

"Too bad she wears that long skirt down to her ankles. It hampers her play. But that's the latest fashion."

"Her parents would be shocked if she wore anything else," Frank added. "Say, she's chasing that puck a long way. The ice isn't very thick where she's going."

Suddenly there was a shattering sound, like milk bottles falling on a cement floor. They heard a scream. Marlene had disappeared from sight.

"She's fallen in!" Max yelled. "Turn the sleigh, Jim! We've got to help her!"

Jim quickly guided the sleigh close—but not too close—to the hole in the ice where Marlene had fallen through. Her head bobbed to the surface. "Help me!" she wailed, "Someone help me!"

Max leaped out carrying one of Frank McGee's spare hockey sticks he'd found in the sleigh. He moved quickly but cautiously toward the hole in the ice. Several of Marlene's companions skated up beside him and skidded to a stop.

"Stay back!" shouted Max. "The ice is thin. Any closer and you'll all fall in!"

Max flopped to the ice and, using his elbows, slowly pushed himself along on his stomach toward the hole.

"Hang onto my feet, Frankie!" he called over his shoulder. McGee grabbed both of Max's ankles firmly.

Max reached out with the stick until it was over the hole.

"Grab the stick blade, miss," he ordered. "Stay calm! I'll have you out in a minute but you must listen to me. Grab the stick!"

The young woman, panicky and almost hysterical, heard the calming words and did as Max directed. She lunged at the stick and clasped it in both hands.

"Hurry!" she gasped. "My long skirt is dragging me down."

Max eased slowly backwards on the ice. "Pull, Frankie! Pull!" he said. Jim McGee and Marty edged forward to assist.

"Stay back!" Max shouted. "There'll be too much weight. Frankie will have to pull us out by himself."

Max was surprised at McGee's strength. His muscular arms and strong hands and wrists were more than strong enough for the job. Slowly, Max and Frankie eased Marlene from the frigid waters. They dragged her across the thin ice to safety.

She lay on the ice, shivering, barely conscious. "Thank you, young man. You . . . you saved my life," she stammered.

"We've got to get her home to Government House," Jim McGee said. "Get her up! Get her in the sleigh! Put a blanket around her! Max and Marty, huddle next to her. Your body heat will help keep her warm."

Jim snapped the reins and the sleigh flew down

the lane to Government House, home of Lord Grey—the Governor General and the King of England's Representative in the Dominion—and Lady Grey.

Servants saw them coming and—sensing the dire emergency—rushed to the sleigh.

"Get her indoors!" Max directed them. "And call a doctor!"

He helped the servants assist Lady Marlene to the threshold. Then others rushed forward to help carry the shivering girl upstairs. Max couldn't think of anything more he could do. Slowly, he went back and sat in the sleigh with his companions.

A few anxious minutes passed. Then the door to Government House opened and a well-dressed, middle-aged couple approached the sleigh. A furry dog loped at their side.

"It's the Governor General and his wife," Frank whispered.

"Hello, Frankie," Governor General Grey said in greeting.

Max was surprised. Apparently everyone in Ottawa, in every social stratum, knew the great Frankie McGee.

"How can I ever thank you for saving our daughter from drowning? She was conscious enough to give us the bare details."

"Is she going to be all right, sir?" Frank asked. "We

didn't want to leave until we were sure."

"She'll be fine. She said to tell you you're not the only hockey player in town who bounces right back up. I'm sure you know she idolizes you, Frankie. Never misses one of your games."

He turned knowingly to Max. "By the way, she had special praise for a certain young man who used a hockey stick to pull her out."

"That would be my brother, sir," Marty said, pointing proudly at Max.

"Indeed? Max, is it?" the Governor General said, pumping Max by the hand. "You're quite the hero, young man. Thank you, thank you and thank you again."

"Thank you, sir. I'm just glad we were able to save her."

"Won't you come in?" Lady Grey asked. "Forgive us for leaving you out here in the cold."

"Thank you, ma'am," Frank McGee said. "You go and look after your daughter. We'll be getting home, now that we know she's going to be all right."

"Well, then, come back on Saturday night. We're having a winter party and we'd be honoured if you would attend. All of you."

"That sounds great," Max replied, thinking perhaps he'd get another opportunity to look into the lovely eyes of Lady Marlene.

"We'll be there," agreed Marty eagerly. "Your

house is ten times the size of our house in Indian River."

"Then it's confirmed," the Governor General said, winking at Marty. "Marlene will be delighted to hear you're all coming. And so are we."

They got back in the sleigh and drove along the river road for a mile or two. Finally, Marty broke the silence. "That was a nice dog they had. Frank, my friend has a dog like that back in Indian River. Well, not quite like that one. My friend's dog lost both ears in a fight, it was missing one leg and its tail was chewed off by a bear."

Marty looked over at Max and winked. He waited.

Finally Frank said, "That's interesting, Marty. What was the name of your friend's dog?"

"Lucky!" Marty said, bursting into laughter. Frank joined in.

Then Frank said, "When I first heard that joke a few years ago, the dog you described was also blind in one eye. Guess you left that part out—on my behalf." He tapped his patch and laughed some more.

Marty couldn't resist. "Want to know my friend's name, Frankie?"

"Sure."

"Everybody called him Seven and a Half. When he was born his parents pulled his name from a hat."

CHAPTER 7

IN THE HOME OF
FRANK MCGEE

The McGee household was a busy one and a happy one. There were eight children, all running in different directions. From the looks of it, the last one to the dinner table risked starvation.

Mr. McGee joked, "There are so many of them I sometimes forget their names. Two of the boys thought their names were 'Get Some Wood' and "Get Some More Wood' for the longest time." He cuffed one of the small boys playfully and the lad squealed with pleasure.

Mr. and Mrs. McGee welcomed the Mitchell brothers without a moment's hesitation. It was as if they were expected, like long-lost family.

"May our home always be too small to hold all of our friends," Mrs. McGee said, a lovely Irish lilt in her voice. "We're cramped for space but we'll find a place for you to sleep, probably on a mattress on the floor of Frankie's room," Mrs. McGee said. "Now sit down, me lads, and fill your bellies with some of my famous Irish stew. And a couple of loaves of my homemade bread. Then we'll talk while Frankie takes his pre-game nap."

She pointed a wooden spoon at the Mitchells. "And none of this 'Mrs.' nonsense in my home, you hear? You boys call me Mary."

"And I'm John," said Mr. McGee. He turned to Marty.

"I hear you tell jokes, lad. Let me warn you. There'll be no telling of Irish jokes in this household." He winked at Frank and Max.

"How about an Irish toast?" queried Marty, raising a glass of milk. "Are they allowed?"

"Toasts are allowed," Mr. McGee said. "Toasts are good."

Marty said, "Okay, here goes:

Here's to you and yours
And to mine and ours,
And if mine and ours
Ever come across you and yours,
I hope you and yours will do
As much for mine and ours,
As mine and ours
Have done for you and yours."

Mr. McGee slapped his knee and laughed. "A good

one, boy. Very good. We're going to get along. I can tell you have some Irish in you. Now here's one for you:

> *There are good ships*
> *And there are wood ships,*
> *And ships that sail the sea.*
> *But the best ships are friendships*
> *And may they always be."*

He held up his glass. "May your troubles be as few and far between as my grandmother's teeth," he said to the Mitchell brothers.

Marty clicked glasses with Mr. McGee and came right back with:

> *"May your heart be light and happy,*
> *May your smile be big and wide,*
> *And may your pockets always have*
> *A coin or two inside!"*

"Enough of this nonsense," Mary McGee said. "Enjoy your food."

Later, after Frankie had left the room to take his customary pre-game nap, she cleared a place on the table and proudly leafed through two of Frankie's scrapbooks. "Here's my Frankie, playing his first game for Ottawa in 1903," she said proudly. "It was against Montreal, the Stanley Cup holders."

"Ottawa defeated the Stanley Cup champions by a score of 7-1 last night," read Max. "The lopsided victory featured the sensational work of young Frank McGee, who scored two of the prettiest goals of the season in his big league debut." He looked up at Mrs. McGee, who was beaming.

"Frankie scored fourteen goals in six games that season," she said, "and helped his team win the Stanley Cup twice, first against the Montreal Victorias and then against the Rat Portage Thistles, the Western champions. Go ahead, Max, read it."

According to the clipping Max read, against the Vics, Frank McGee was simply spectacular, even under wretched playing conditions.

"The ice was so soft," Max read aloud, "Ottawa's sensational rookie was forced to skate in water up to his ankles."

"Perhaps they exaggerated by an inch or two," admitted Mrs. McGee. "But it was like a lake. Frankie could have used a paddle in place of a hockey stick."

Jim McGee entered the kitchen and joined the conversation. "That same week, Ottawa played the Thistles and won another series for the Cup. The Thistles took the opener on fast ice. Those boys could skate! But in game two, there were pools of water all over the ice. At one point, the puck fell through a hole in the slush and was never recovered. Perhaps a big fish was swimming under the ice and had it for dinner."

The thought of something so ridiculous made Max and Marty laugh out loud.

Jim grinned and said, "My, but those Thistles were hot. Furious and frustrated. They claimed the rink manager flooded the ice with two inches of water just before game time, even though a warm spell had moved in. The temperature that day was well above freezing."

"Did he flood the ice?" Max asked.

"He sure did. Some of the Ottawa players—but not Frankie, of course—even helped him with the hose. The Thistles couldn't skate on that pond— swim maybe—but the Ottawa boys could. And we kept the Cup."

"But isn't that cheating?" Marty protested.

Mr. McGee shrugged. "You may be right, Marty. Perhaps that's why Frankie refused to help flood the ice. But our fans will say, 'It's not cheating. That's hockey.' When it comes to the Stanley Cup, most teams will do anything to win it."

"Like forcing an opposing team to drop a star player," Jim McGee said, his eyes twinkling. "One of Frankie's teammates—a mediocre player—took a stick in the ribs one night. He dropped to the ice like a stone and had to be carried off. In the dressing room he stripped off his shirt and the trainer dragged a stick blade across his ribs, leaving a long red welt. The trainer called for the referee to come see the injury. The player moaned and groaned and said he could play no more. So the referee instructed the opposing team to drop a player—a good one. And Ottawa went on to win the game."

"Another sneaky move," Marty declared. "But I love these stories."

"You bet it was sneaky," Jim said. "Like Dad said, teams will do anything to win. Some teams encourage kids in the rush end to bring peashooters to the games. They shoot peas at the goalies, goal judges or the referee. Those peas can sting, I tell you. And you can't tell where the peas are coming from. That's why some goalies wear small caps on their heads."

Mr. McGee chuckled. "It also protects them from any pigeons sitting up in the rafters overhead," he said. "Pigeons are full of surprises."

"Yep. They're full of . . . well, surprises," Jim agreed. "Anyway, the following season, Ottawa defended the Cup against challenges from Winnipeg, Toronto, Brandon and a new team from Montreal, the Wanderers. Frankie had a great year, scoring twenty-one goals in eight playoff games."

"Earlier this season, Frankie was almost killed in a game with the Wanderers," Mrs. McGee said. "That brute, Punch Pounder, sneaked up on him and knocked him cold with a whack to the head. It was his way of getting back at Frankie. You see, Pounder stuck Frank in the eye with his stick a couple of years ago in Montreal. Frankie told the newspapers the blow was deliberate. Pounder was suspended. He should have gone to jail." She shook her head sadly. "It was such a mean, vicious thing to do. My son lost his eye . . ." She turned away, bringing her apron to her face to wipe away a tear.

"Pounder may have knocked Frank cold the last time they met but Frankie came back to score three goals against the Wanderers," Jim McGee said. "He likes to retaliate in the best possible way—by showing up the opposition."

Max picked up a recent clipping. "The Ottawa Citizen calls that game when Frank was knocked out 'an incredible, unforgettable display of sheer butchery.'" He continued reading, "'Play was so brutal the referee stopped to don a hard hat. McGee was the playoff season's best scorer with seventeen goals in six games.'"

"The ref wore a hard hat?" Marty interrupted. "Like a construction worker?"

"That's right," said Jim.

"You've sure got a lot of clippings," Marty observed. "Wow! Here's one from 1899."

Jim McGee laughed when he saw it. "Hard to believe, isn't it? What a story! The referee—fellow named Findlay—lost his temper in a Stanley Cup game at Montreal. He was mad at the players because they defied him. Just plain ignored him. So he took off his skates and went home. Left four thousand people sitting in the stands and the players standing around on the ice, wondering what to do next.

"Team officials chased after Findlay in a sleigh and finally persuaded him to come back. But by then the players in both clubs had enough and had left the rink. They'd waited over an hour for the ref," chuckled Jim, "and so had most of the fans. It's the only playoff game for the Cup with no ending."

"Couldn't they find another referee?" Marty asked.

"You'd think so. But they didn't. Nope. The game was never finished. True story."

Jim McGee laughed, thinking of another hockey tale. "One time, the Silver Seven were in Montreal for a big game. Hundreds of fans had lined up outside the arena and had waited for hours for the gates to open. When the ticket sellers didn't open their windows on time, the fans became enraged. They stormed the building and broke down the doors and smashed the windows. They barged inside the arena and occupied all the best seats. They saw a playoff game without having to pay a cent."

"Another true story," confirmed Mrs. McGee. "It's here in my scrapbooks somewhere, along with the story of Chummy Hill, a Toronto player who scored a Stanley Cup goal in Winnipeg—with half a puck."

"Half a puck!" snorted Marty. "How did that happen?"

"Toronto was playing Winnipeg for the Cup three seasons ago. During the game, the puck split into two wee pieces. Hill belted one o' the chunks of rubber into the Winnipeg goal. The referee allowed the goal and Toronto won the game 5-3."

Marty chuckled. "The score should have been 5 to two and a half," he said.

Just then, Frankie came into the kitchen, looking refreshed, ready for the big game.

"Had a little pre-game nap," he said, giving his mother a kiss on the cheek. "You coming to the game tonight, Mum?"

"Not on yer life, son. You know I can't bear to watch you play against that devil from Montreal."

"Punch Pounder? Mom, I'll skate him dizzy. Hey! Did I hear someone spouting poetry while I was in the bedroom?"

"You did, son. I know how you love the written word. And so do I. Have you got a new one for me?"

"How about this one?" Frankie quipped, clearing his throat,

"May love and laughter light your days
And warm your heart and home.
May good and faithful friends be yours
Wherever you may roam.
May peace and plenty bless your world

With joy that long endures.
May all life's passing seasons
Bring the best to you and yours."

Frankie's mother applauded. She said, "I like that one, son. Who wrote it?"

"It's by Anon Neemus, Mom."

"Never heard of him," she said, frowning.

Jim burst out laughing.

"Mom, don't you get it? Anonymous?"

"You're a little devil, Frankie," she scolded, slapping his wrist. "Foolin' me like that."

Frankie gave her a big hug and kissed her on the cheek. "Sorry, Mum."

He turned to Max and Marty. "Let's go, men," he said. "We'll get the sleigh hitched up."

CHAPTER 8

PLAYING THE WANDERERS

There was a huge crowd outside Dey's arena. It was an hour before game time and many had been there all afternoon. And most, it appeared, were clamouring for tickets. Clusters of fans surrounded busy scalpers shouting, "I'll buy! I'll buy! What's your price?"

A young man bolted from the crowd and took the reins of the sleigh from Frank McGee. McGee tipped him generously. "See you after the game, Shorty."

"You mean after the win," Shorty said. He eyed the Mitchell brothers. "You boys playing tonight?"

"No, not us," Max said.

"Not unless the Silver Seven need us," corrected Marty boldly.

"That'll be the frosty Friday," Shorty brayed. "Why, Frankie here could whip those Wanderers all by hisself."

Max and Marty followed the McGees through a

throng of backslapping fans and supporters and into the arena through the players' entrance.

McGee handed the Mitchell brothers two tickets—rinkside seats next to the penalty box.

The arena filled quickly with noisy fans, among them a trainload from Montreal, numbering about five hundred. Some of the Montrealers carried megaphones they could use to shout insults at the Ottawa players and the referee. Taunting erupted immediately. Tempers flared and a few scuffles broke out, but policemen were on hand to quickly intervene.

"This is exciting," Marty said, standing to see. "I never dreamed early day fans could get so emotional over a hockey game."

In the rush end—an area of standing room at fifty cents per ticket—fans elbowed each other roughly for a good view. There was some good-natured pushing and shoving until tempers flared. Punches were thrown and noses were bloodied. Once again, busy policemen hustled over to calm the crowd.

"Sometimes the safest place to be at a hockey game is on the ice," Max observed sagely.

A huge roar filled the arena as a red carpet was thrown down and the Governor General stepped out to "face" the puck.

His duty done, he retreated to a private box, not far from where the Mitchell boys were sitting.

"There's Lady Marlene," Marty cried, pointing.

"Hi, Marlene, I mean Lady Marlene!" he shouted, waving madly to catch her attention.

"Sit down, Marty," Max said, as heads turned. "Show some manners, some respect."

Lady Marlene had heard Marty's greeting and flashed the Mitchells a winning smile.

"She's gorgeous . . . when she's all dressed up," said Max.

"And when she's not drowning," quipped Marty.

"I'll grant you that," Max said. "Nobody much looks their best when they're drowning." He flashed a return smile and waved.

"Hey, show some respect," Marty said, poking Max in the ribs with an elbow. "Now watch the game."

Mr. Smeaton, the referee, resplendent in his Sunday suit, shirt and tie and derby hat, selected two men from the crowd to act as goal judges. They scrambled eagerly onto the ice and took their places, one behind each net. Each was handed a white flag that he was to wave if the puck entered the net.

The referee skated to centre ice where he "faced" the puck by placing it between the sticks of the opposing centremen. Then he rang his bell, at the same time pulling his fingers back deftly just before the clashing sticks could crack his knuckles.

"Why doesn't he just toss the puck in?" Marty asked Max.

"I'm sure he will—in time," Max replied. "A broken finger will teach him that."

The contest, played in two halves, was spectacular. Both teams boasted skilled skaters and shooters. The goaltenders, despite their flimsy equipment, were superb. Ottawa scored first but the Wanderers quickly tied the score.

Then Punch Pounder took two penalties in a row, both times for infractions against McGee.

Late in the first half, with Pounder in the box, McGee spun away from a check and, with a tremendous burst of speed, broke in on the Montreal goal. He pulled the goalie one way, then went the other and whipped the puck into the net.

Goal!

"He deked him!" Max shouted. "Did you see? He deked him!"

"You taught him that move, Max. He's a fast learner. Go, Frankeeeee!"

McGee scored two more goals in the second half, both times waltzing around big Punch Pounder and making him look foolish. On both goals, McGee skated in from a sharp angle, whipped behind the net, popped out on the other side, and tucked the puck inside the far post.

"Uncle Jake's move!" Marty whooped in glee. "He did it better than you do it, Max."

Max laughed. "You're right, Marty. You said he

was a fast learner."

After his third goal, Frankie skated past Pounder and impishly reached out with the blade of his stick, plucking the little black cap Pounder wore off his head, revealing a prominent bald spot. The fans howled with mirth. But Pounder was furious and slammed his stick against the goal net. "I'll get you yet, Frankie," he threatened. "You little weasel!"

Some Wanderers fans at rinkside supported Pounder and shouted insults at McGee through their megaphones. But referee Smeaton quickly silenced McGee's critics. He ended their tirade by cracking them over the heads with his bell. When a noisy fan used his megaphone to bellow an obscenity in his ear, Smeaton turned and grabbed the device. He threw it on the ice and crushed it with his skate, much to the delight of the Ottawa fans.

A few minutes later, McGee's flashing blades carried him between the Montreal defenders. He burst into the clear and once again pulled the Montreal netminder with a nifty deke—and scored. The goal judge, standing on the ice behind the net, waved his white flag. The crowd erupted, celebrating McGee's fourth goal.

McGee's rush carried him right into the fans sitting behind the low boards. They embraced him and hugged him. They laughed and patted his back. But when they released him and he turned to skate away, trouble was waiting.

Big Punch Pounder could take no more. He ploughed into the surprised McGee and knocked him flat on his backside. He began to pummel the Ottawa star with his big fists. Wisely, McGee covered up, protecting his good eye.

Then, somehow, McGee squirmed out from under his much bigger opponent and regained his feet. The crowd roared and applauded. He waited sportingly until Pounder also rose to his feet. Then McGee moved in, his fists flying. One, two, three punches bloodied Pounder's face. Four, five, six punches and Pounder began to fall. He tumbled on his back. McGee leaped on top of him. McGee's furious attack brought another huge roar from the crowd.

"McGee! McGee! McGee!" the fans bellowed.

"What a licking!" Marty howled. "Give it to him, Frankie!"

But the fight was over. Frank McGee gathered his stick and gloves from the ice and skated to the penalty box. He sat there, breathing hard, staring straight ahead. Then, slowly, he turned his head and glanced over at the Mitchell brothers. The hint of a smile moved to his lips and he winked.

By then big Pounder had staggered to his feet. He weaved his way to the penalty box where he used a small towel to wipe the blood from his ruddy face. He sat a few feet from McGee, a burly police constable between them.

Pounder appeared to have had enough. So did his teammates, who realized they were in for a crushing defeat.

The game continued and soon the two players in the box were all but forgotten. But not by Max. He noticed Pounder examining the blade of his stick, which had been split during the battle on the ice.

"Marty, look!" Max said, pointing. "Pounder's stick has a jagged point. He can't come back and play with it. Too dangerous."

"What's he doing?" asked Marty.

Pounder had leaned over, as if to tie a loose skatelace. Suddenly he raised his stick in both hands and, leaping across the policeman, lunged at McGee. The pointed blade was aimed directly at McGee's good eye.

Marty jumped to his feet. "Look out! Frankie, look out!"

Max had dashed from his seat, however, and flew at Pounder like a bulldog, knocking him sprawling with a flying tackle. Pounder's stick sailed high in the air, his knees buckled and he went down in a heap.

Frank McGee, who'd been watching the flow of action on the ice, wasn't aware of how close he'd come to being blinded. Only when he turned to see Max fly to his rescue did he realize Pounder's deadly intent.

By then the referee was there, ringing his bell to

stop the play. "Yer outta the game, Pounder! Get to your dressing room!"

Two policemen escorted Pounder across the ice, threatening to charge him with assault. The Ottawa fans booed Pounder mercilessly—and threatened him too—but from a safe distance.

Max picked himself up, dusted himself off, and returned to his seat. He heard a wave of applause sweep through the stands, then a roar of appreciation. He turned to Marty. "Who are they applauding?" he asked, looking around. "Is it McGee?"

"Not this time. It's you, you goofball," Marty told him. "You've just made five thousand friends by saving the sight of One-Eyed Frank McGee. Even the Governor General is applauding you."

Max turned to see if it was true. But when he saw Lady Marlene standing and waving in his direction, the Governor General and all others were forgotten.

He gave her a small wave in return. "She has the nicest eyes," he murmured dreamily. "And a perfect smile."

"Oh, brother," Marty replied. "Max, are you feeling all right? Did Pounder whack you on the head?"

Max grinned. "Marty, I've never felt better."

Marty shook his head. "Just remember. She's not like the girls back home. Lady Marlene is almost . . . almost royalty."

CHAPTER 9

A PARTY AT
GOVERNMENT HOUSE

Lord Earl Grey, like his predecessors Lords Stanley and Aberdeen, recognized the importance of sport in the thriving Dominion of Canada. At Government House, or Rideau Hall as it was often called, his staff maintained a large outdoor ice rink for skating parties and impromptu hockey games. A team called the Rideau Hall Rebels played there. It was a team originally organized by the sons of Lord Stanley.

Lord Stanley's daughter, Lady Isobel, and her friend Lulu LeMoine, were among the earliest females to take up the game. Wearing long white skirts, colourful scarves and hats, with white mittens serving as hockey gloves, they would play once or twice a week. No men allowed.

It was Lady Stanley who was credited with introducing a defensive ploy to the game—that of crouching down in front of her team's goalie. The long skirts worn by her and her teammates would fan out along the ice and opposing players found it almost impossible to skim a shot through to the goal.

There were other winter games and pastimes to pursue at Government House.

Guests were encouraged to hike through the nearby woods on skis and snowshoes. There was a thrilling toboggan slide on the grounds. And one could always assist in the building of an ice castle, using large blocks of ice cut from the nearby river.

There were gala parties at Christmas, and dinner dances. Many involved skating races and the joy of ice dancing.

When the McGees and the Mitchells arrived in their sleigh that Saturday night, they noted the dozens of Japanese lanterns hanging from tree branches, the young skaters already gliding around the rink, a trio of musicians on the veranda, and the maids and servants that appeared to be everywhere.

The guests surrounded Frank McGee when he stepped down from the sleigh. They complimented him on his fine play against the Wanderers and his smashing victory over Punch Pounder in the big fight.

He reacted graciously and pumped every extended hand. He told his fans he might well be in the hospital if it hadn't been for the prompt actions of his new friends, Max and Marty Mitchell.

The Mitchell brothers beamed. They were proud of Frank McGee, proud of the man known as "the world's greatest hockey player."

The guests had been urged to bring their skates. Those who had, changed quickly in a large change house next to the rink. There they were hailed by Lord Grey and Lady Marlene, who were about to take a few turns around the ice.

"I won't stay long on these blades," Lord Grey stated. "I've got weak ankles, you know."

When he glided away on wobbly legs, Max turned to Marty. "Have you ever noticed how everyone who can't skate well claims to have weak ankles?"

Marty snickered. "It's a good excuse for getting off the ice," he said. "I notice Lady Marlene has very nice ankles. I bet they're not weak."

They weren't. Lady Marlene was an excellent skater and when Max glided onto the ice, she offered her hand. They skated gracefully around and around. Max couldn't recall ever having a better time on the ice—without a hockey stick in his hands. They moved closer together and Max put an arm around her waist. But when he looked across the ice and saw Lord Grey standing at rinkside, staring at them thoughtfully, he said, "Perhaps we'd better go inside."

Light from the swaying Japanese lanterns danced in her hair. Her violet eyes sparkled. "All right," she said, her lips close to his. "I'm famished. There'll be more skating later. But before we go I must tell you, Max, the past few moments have been the most enjoyable I've experienced since we came to Canada."

Max was thrilled with the compliment. He became flustered and could think of no suitable reply. Impulsively, he pulled her toward him. He gave her a hug and kissed her cool cheek. But not before he looked to make sure Lord Grey had turned his back.

The dinner, while informal, was grand, with a variety of delicacies that had Marty drooling with delight. The Mitchell brothers were honoured when they were invited to sit at the Governor General's table. Max quickly slipped into a chair next to Lady Marlene. His choice of seats did not go unnoticed for both Frank and Jim gave him a "thumbs up" and knowing smiles.

There was one embarrassing moment. Marty reached for a sweet roll and when he leaned forward he broke wind. He bolted from his chair and ran for the men's room. Lady Marlene tried to ignore Marty's *faux pas* but failed. She burst into giggles. Max looked up at the chandelier and rolled his eyes.

When Marty returned and slipped back into his chair, Lady Marlene impishly asked him, "Want another sweet roll, Marty?"

"No thanks," he said sheepishly.

After the meal, a bell tinkled and Lord Grey rose to welcome his guests. He paid special homage to Frank McGee, saying, "My friend Mr. McGee—indeed he is everybody's friend—played a sparkling game of hockey last night at the arena and almost single-handedly humbled the mighty Wanderers. He personifies all that is right with hockey: grit, determination, skill on skates and a high degree of sportsmanship, ahem, his fisticuffs with Mr. Pounder notwithstanding."

His guests chuckled at his reference to Frank's one-sided confrontation with Pounder. They knew that McGee rarely fought. But when he did he fought hard.

"Mr. McGee might have been badly injured in last night's battle had it not been for the quick thinking of his friends, Max and Marty Mitchell, who are with us tonight. Newcomers to the city, they have already distinguished themselves—Max in particular—for bravely defending Mr. McGee from Mr. Pounder's cowardly attack."

Lord Grey's words prompted a round of applause and shouts of, "Bravo, Max!"

Lord Grey continued. "The courage of these young men and the McGee brothers, as you all must know by now, resulted in a rescue from drowning of our precious daughter Marlene after she fell through the ice. I am convinced that Max—with Marty, Frank and Jim assisting—saved our Marlene from certain death."

There was wild applause from every table. The brothers squirmed and blushed until it was over. Max felt a hand grip his under the tablecloth—Lady Marlene's. His face became still redder and he didn't dare look in her direction.

Lord Grey had some final words. "At times I wish I had been Governor General a few years ago—in Lord Stanley's time. For then I would have donated a trophy to hockey and it would have been called the Grey Cup. But Lord Stanley beat me to it. So I am announcing a similar trophy, donated by my family and me—to the sport of football. It is to be called the Grey Cup."

There was more applause, for football was extremely popular in the nation's capital. In fact, Frank McGee—a speedy halfback—was the captain of the Ottawa team.

"Now let us don skates and enjoy some merriment outdoors," Lord Grey suggested. He explained that the highlight of the evening would be the traditional skating race: ten laps around the rink—with a prize of $25 going to the winner. Frank McGee had been champion for four years running.

"Perhaps sometime in this century you will meet your match," Lord Grey chided Frank, "before your ankles grow weak like mine. But there appears to be no challenger on the horizon who can surpass your swiftness over the ice."

All of the guests laughed and applauded. They rose to don warmer clothing and moved outdoors.

Max and Marty took turns skating with Lady Marlene. Then both skated with Lulu LeMoine, one of Ottawa's finest female hockey players. Lulu appeared to be reluctant to let Max go once the music ended. "We must play hockey together one day soon," she told him. "I'll give you my address."

"Lulu is such a flirt," Lady Marlene said when they returned to her side. "Oh, by the way, please call me Marlene. 'Lady' is a bit stuffy and formal, don't you think? But the Royal Family in England insists on it."

Before long, an aide to Lord Grey, shouting through a megaphone, called the male skaters to take their places for the Big Race. Small metal posts had been hammered into the ice to mark the boundaries of the racecourse. The distance was ten laps, almost a mile. Guests rushed forward to get the best vantage places.

"Come on, Max, let's go," Marty urged, pulling Max to the starting line. "Let's see if we can beat Frank."

"Not much chance of that," Max retorted. "He's fast as a fox with his tail on fire. And he's in terrific shape."

A bell clanged and the skaters charged across the ice—about a dozen in all. Frank McGee sprinted to the lead, with his brother Jim close behind. Max and Marty settled back in third and fourth place.

Max began to feel elated. The joy of skating filled his being and he accelerated, lengthening his steady, fluid strides. On lap five, he overtook and passed Jim McGee, skirting him smoothly to the outside.

Frank looked over his shoulder and laughed. He loved the challenge he faced from Max. He shouted, "Nice move, kid. But you won't pass me. Here I go!"

McGee's flashing skates dug into the hard ice and he sprinted even faster.

People watching were amazed. "He's like a cannon-ball on skates," one of them said in awe.

"But look!" said another, "The young Mitchell lad is staying right with him."

Two laps to go and noisy applause and cheering rose into the winter air. The finish to the race promised to be the closest in history. For once McGee was facing a challenger who would not wilt.

One lap to skate and Max had moved up slightly on his friend. He was almost in McGee's moving shadow. With a hundred yards to the finish line, Max took a deep breath and urged his burning legs to move even faster. The two men were even now and McGee was no longer laughing. His reputation was at stake and he too sprinted hard to the finish line. But Max flashed across the tape inches in front, then coasted along, head down, his hands on his knees. He felt someone nudge his shoulder.

"That was a great race, kid. You're a marvel." It was McGee, ever the sportsman. Max was able to stammer, "Thanks, Frank. We both hate to lose, eh? But you're the champion in my eyes, the best competitor I've ever seen. I call the race a tie."

"No, it wasn't a tie," McGee snorted. "You beat me fair and square, but not by much." He raised Max's arm and turned to the crowd. "Let's hear it for the fastest man on ice—Max Mitchell!"

The guests applauded and cheered.

McGee had some final words of advice for Max.

"We've both been blessed with strong bodies and lots of athletic ability. So we've known the joy of winning. And we hate losing. But when we lose, as we all must do at times, it's important to lose gracefully. And important to congratulate and praise the player or team that beats you. That's what sportsmanship is all about."

"I know what you mean and I'll remember your words," Max replied. He paused for a moment then said straight-faced.

"There's only one other player I've met who can match you for fair play, gentlemanly conduct and all round sportsmanship, Frankie."

McGee looked puzzled. "And who would that be?"

"My hockey idol, of course," Max said, his eyes twinkling mischievously, "Punch Pounder."

Max raced away laughing but not before Frank McGee slapped him hard across his backside.

CHAPTER 10

THE CUP SHOWS UP

"Is that what I think it is?" Marty said in awe. "Is that really the Stanley Cup?" He pointed to a small silver trophy resting on a bench in the Ottawa dressing room.

"It is indeed," Frank McGee said. "Harvey Pulford lugged it back from Montreal after we won it there. He threw it in his bedroom closet and forgot about it. He was looking for some old boots to wear the other day and stumbled over the Cup. He figured it was somebody else's turn to look after it so I volunteered."

"If you take it home your mom will put flowers in it," Max said.

"She probably will," Frankie chuckled.

"And your dad will use it as a spittoon," Marty predicted.

"He'd better not. It's the most coveted trophy in hockey. Lord Stanley donated it but the poor fellow never got to see a playoff game for the Cup. He was recalled to England before a Cup game was played. He was a big fan of the Ottawa club."

Max approached the Cup and peered into the bowl. "I'm surprised it's all scratched up," he observed.

"What!" Frankie exploded. He rushed over to take a closer look. He held the bowl up to the light. "Why, you're right. Those little buggers! I'd like to strangle them."

"You mean the Wanderers?" asked Marty. "What did they do?"

"They've ruined the inside of the bowl. They've scratched names in there with a nail or something. In big letters! And some of the names are from last year's team. Those rascals! There's not much room left for any other names. Now we'll have to ask permission to have the bowl re-silvered."

"Why not just replace the trophy?" Marty suggested. "Just order another one."

"No, Marty. Never. This Cup is the original and holds too much meaning for too many people. With luck, teams will be scrapping over this Cup when I'm old and toothless."

"Then it will need some additional space for the names of winning players," Max said. "A large base for it might be a good idea."

"Good thinking, Max. I'll mention it to the Cup

trustees." He howled when he noticed a familiar name inside the bowl. "Look! Punch Pounder scratched his name in letters an inch high. Oh, I hope the trustees slap the Wanderers with a whopping big fine for this. Imagine defacing the Cup."

"Frank, I can't believe you play so many Stanley Cup matches," Max said. "Seems to me once a season is enough. But Ottawa seems to defend the Cup almost every few days."

"That's why they call it a challenge trophy, Max. A lot of teams are eager to take it away from us. We won it from Montreal last season—1903—playing late in the season. The ice was covered in pools of water.

"Our next challenge—early this season—comes from the Winnipeg Rowing Club. If we win that series—and we should—we meet the Toronto Marlboros. After that comes our toughest challenge—a rematch with our bitter rivals—the high-scoring Wanderers. One season they averaged ten goals per game. I insist that you and Marty be my guests for these challenges. The fellows say you bring us luck."

"We may have to stay around," Marty said, a twinkle in his eye. "Your mother says she's going to adopt us. Even if we're not Irish. I like Mary. She laughs at all my jokes."

"Well, she's a tolerant woman," agreed Frankie,

nudging Max and winking.

"I told her the one about the Irishman who went to the theatre to be entertained by a ventriloquist," said Marty. "The ventriloquist and his dummy friend kept making jokes about ignorant hockey players. Finally, the hockey player stood up and yelled out, 'I resent all those wisecracks about stupid hockey players.'

"The ventriloquist said, 'Sir, they're only jokes.'

"The hockey player said angrily, 'You be quiet. I'm not talking to you. I'm talking to that little guy sitting on your knee.'"

Frankie laughed. "That's a good one," he said. "How did Mom react?"

"She groaned and rolled her eyes. But I know she liked it."

"Frankie, we'll stay around," said Max. "We don't want to miss those Stanley Cup games coming up. It's the chance of a lifetime."

A few days later, Max and Marty attended the first game of a best-of-three series against the Winnipeg Rowing Club. "Look at that!" mused Marty. Someone—the rink manager, perhaps—had painted a thin line across the goalmouth, connecting the posts.

"Now that's more like it," Marty said.

The Silver Seven won the opener 9–1, lost the second game 6–2, and captured the deciding game—a thrilling 2–0 shutout. At the bell, fans leaped over the boards and hoisted the Silver Seven to their shoulders, celebrating their Stanley Cup victory.

Less than a month later, Frank McGee sparkled in a two-game series against the Toronto Marlboros. He scored three goals in the first game and five in the second. The Silver Seven won by scores of 6–3 and 11–2. Once again, there was pandemonium in the arena and another mammoth celebration.

Ottawa then travelled by train to Montreal, where they met their toughest challengers—the Wanderers. Max and Marty—the good luck charms—were invited along. They were disappointed when the two clubs finished the first game with the scored tied 5–5.

The referee, "Doc" Kearns, ordered overtime but the Wanderers, led by Punch Pounder, protested. Pounder was furious, insisting the final goal that tied the score should not have counted.

"The puck didn't cross the line," he fumed. "We ain't playin' overtime, Kearns," Pounder snarled. "Yer a lousy official! That's it. I ain't playing another minute until we get a new ref."

Kearns said, "Fine with me, Pounder. I've seen enough of you, too." He took off his skates, threw on his overcoat, and went home in his sleigh.

"Pounder's such a fool," McGee commented when the Ottawa boys were settled in their seats back on the train, headed for home. "The Wanderers were one goal away from winning and they let Pounder toss that chance away because he thought the referee was biased."

On the following day, the Stanley Cup trustees met and ordered the two clubs to start the series all over again. Both games would be played in Ottawa. Pounder blew up again and convinced his mates to ignore the decision.

"We never get a fair deal in Ottawa," he complained. "The referees there don't like us. It's clear to me that all they want to do is protect their 'boy,' McGee. Well, I won't have it." The Wanderers withdrew their challenge.

Another team quickly took their place. Playing in Ottawa didn't bother some brash young men from Brandon, Manitoba. Billing themselves as the Western champions, the Brandon boys showed up in Ottawa for a two-game series, vowing to surprise McGee with a few Western tricks. "He doesn't scare us," their coach said confidently. "He steps into his pants one leg at a time—just like my boys do."

"Frankie skated them dizzy," Marty chuckled after the series. "What a scorer! He scored five goals in the opener and three more in game two." The Silver Seven won by scores of 6–3 and 9–3.

The season ended in March when a sudden warm spell melted the ice in Dey's Arena. No more challenges were possible. The Silver Seven retained the Stanley Cup.

The Mitchell brothers spent the off-season in Ottawa. Frankie took them golfing—a new game for them—and laughed when Marty lost 12 balls over the first nine holes.

He took them canoeing and camping along the Rideau River. His friends Yvon Delisle and Andre Savard taught them how to converse in passable French. Max and Marty played endless games of road hockey, honing their skills.

One day Frankie brought the Stanley Cup home and placed it on the dining room table.

"The boys asked me to look after it for the rest of the summer," he explained. "Now Mom can put her flowers in it."

"Better take good care of it," Max cautioned him, speaking with authority. "It's going to be around for another hundred years or more."

"It is? How do you know that?" Frankie asked.

Max hesitated. "Uh," he improvised hastily. "Just a feeling." He added sheepishly, "Sometimes I think I can predict the future."

"Really? You hiding a crystal ball under the bed upstairs?"

Max chuckled. "No, nothing like that, Frankie. It's just a . . . well, a feeling."

"Oh, yeah? And what do you see in the future for me?"

Max hesitated again. He knew the history of the

Stanley Cup but he didn't know a thing about Frankie's future. He took a deep breath. Suddenly, he felt a sharp pain in his chest. A blurred image of a terrible tragedy. A nation mourning. A family devastated. He shook his head slightly, and the image vanished as abruptly as it had appeared. Perhaps the Little People had been trying to send him a message.

He said shakily, "Oh, I'm sure you've got a bright future, Frankie. Everybody loves you. You could be Mayor of Ottawa someday. Or sit in Parliament. Maybe even become Canada's Prime Minister."

McGee laughed out loud. "Thanks, Max. So you don't think I'm just another dumb hockey player—like the one who shouted at the ventriloquist?"

"Far from it, Frankie. You're smart. You've got lots of leadership ability. People respect you. I see you doing great things with your life." Once again, Max was shaken with a moment of fear, fear for his friend's safety. But again, the feeling vanished in an instant. He tried to make light of his concern, not wishing to upset the hockey star. "All you have to do is get past a big conflict that'll test you, Frankie. But don't worry. That's somewhere far off in the future."

"Well, I'd like to contribute something to society, like my uncle D'Arcy McGee did," Frankie said. "My uncle was a great politician—devoted to improving life for Canadians—until a crazed gunman assassinated him. I hope you don't see somebody in

Ottawa taking a shot at me in the future."

"No, no, nobody in Ottawa would do that," Max assured him. But he found it hard to shake the image of a huge black cloud he saw in McGee's distant future.

CHAPTER 11

GREETING THE BOYS
FROM THE YUKON

A new season of hockey began in December when winter winds howled and the ice in Dey's Arena set hard and slick.

One January morning, McGee woke the Mitchell brothers and told them to get dressed.

"We're going to meet the train from the West," he said. "The team from Dawson City has finally arrived in town. They've travelled four thousand miles to challenge us for the Cup. There's never been a challenge like it and the entire city is talking about it. Let's go meet the team they call the Nuggets."

They arrived at Union Station just in time. The train from Vancouver had pulled in and the players from the far-off Yukon—all seven of them—stepped down.

"My, they look tired," Marty observed, watching the visitors stretch their legs and arms.

"They should be tired," said Frankie. "They left Dawson City on December 19. They've been on the road for almost a month—and with no chance to practice. I feel sorry for them already."

"The Great McGee feeling sorry for an opponent," Max said. "That's something new."

"I must be getting soft in my old age," Frank replied. "Seriously, I give them credit. I hear some of them started out on their bicycles. Imagine that! When the bicycles broke down they tossed them aside and hitched a ride with some dogsledders. Others walked the trail to Whitehorse. Must be over three hundred miles."

"Did they take the train the rest of the way?" Marty asked.

"Heck, no. They took a train to Skagway. That's on the coast of Alaska. By then they were way behind schedule and they missed their ship to Vancouver. They had no choice but to seek passage on a tramp steamer headed to Seattle in Washington State. From Seattle they boarded a train to Vancouver and then hopped on another train headed for Ottawa. See what I mean? Some hockey players will do anything for a chance to grab the Stanley Cup."

Just then, a teenager stepped down from the train and looked around. He spotted Frank McGee in the crowd and headed toward him, a big smile on his face.

"Who's that coming? Their stickboy?" Marty asked.

"It's their goaltender," McGee said in a whisper. "He's only seventeen. Name's Forrest. Albert Forrest."

Albert Forrest took off his peaked cap and introduced himself to McGee. "I'm a big fan of yours, Mr. McGee," he said, respectfully. "It's a real honour to meet you and a great thrill to find myself playing against you."

"Thanks, Albert," McGee said. "I've heard good things about you, too. How in the world did you talk your parents into letting you come all this way to play a couple of hockey games?"

"It wasn't easy, sir. I persuaded them it would be a once-in-a-lifetime opportunity. Very educational. And I had to promise them I'd bring back the Stanley Cup. Oh, yes. And that I wouldn't let you score any goals."

McGee laughed. "I wish I could tell you I'd make it easy for you to keep that promise. But I can't. Here in Ottawa we've grown very fond of the Cup. We're not going to give it up without a fight. As for scoring goals, sometimes I think that's what I was put on Earth to do, Albert. So be ready."

Marty nudged McGee. "How about some breakfast, Frankie? The Russell House has a breakfast special for fifteen cents. Perhaps Albert can join us."

"I'd love to," Albert Forrest said. "We're staying at the Russell. I'll check in with my teammates. Then I'll meet you in the dining room."

Over bacon and eggs, toast and coffee, Max and Marty plied Albert with questions about the Yukon and the recent gold rush there that had attracted thousands of hopeful prospectors and dreamers to a remote place in the far North.

"Only a few people got rich," Albert told them. "By the time everyone got there, most of the mines had been staked. Most of the money wound up in the pockets of a few.

"But those who became millionaires spent money to build an indoor arena and an indoor swimming pool," he added. "And a ball park. Because the sun never sets in summer we could play baseball at midnight. You won't see that anywhere else."

"Do you have a good hockey team?" Max asked. "Think you can take the Cup away from Ottawa?"

"Perhaps we can—if we can find a way to stop Mr. McGee," Albert replied tactfully. "We don't know how good we are because we've never played any top calibre teams. And we're sadly out of shape because we haven't been on skates in almost a month. And our best player—Weldy Young—couldn't leave with us because of his job in the Yukon Government. He's trying to get here in time for a game or two. But I doubt that he'll be in the line-up for the first game tomorrow."

Marty was eager to ask Albert about life in Dawson City during the famous gold rush of '98.

"Did you find any gold? Are there lots of million-aires up there? Do you live in igloos?"

Albert laughed. "No, we don't live in igloos. They are the homes of Eskimos, who live many miles north of Dawson City. When we first arrived in Dawson we lived in tents. Now we live in a log house. And my family never got rich. My father wasn't as lucky as some of the others. A few prospectors became millionaires, but not many. Most men made the hard journey there and back without much to show for it except great memories, or in some cases, shattered dreams."

"Tell us about some of the people who won for-tunes," Marty said.

Albert munched on a sweet roll and smiled. "My father's friend, Charley Anderson, became known as 'The Lucky Swede.' Charley got drunk one night and paid every cent he had—eight hundred dollars—for a claim some stranger sold him. When he sobered up the next morning, he figured he'd made a dreadful mistake and tried to get his money back. But the stranger had left town. So Charley had little choice but to work his claim, one he thought was worth-less. Lo and behold, he mined over a million dollars in gold from it over the next few months."

"Was it hard to keep law and order in Dawson City?" Max wanted to know.

"The North West Mounted Police kept the law and there wasn't much crime," Albert said. "It was different in Skagway, which is a seaport in Alaska, part of the United States. In Skagway, a notorious swindler named Soapy Smith greeted hundreds of prospectors at the dock. Soapy headed up a gang of smooth talkers and tough guys. One of his men even posed as a priest. Soapy's men sold the newcomers supplies and offered to store their goods for them. They pretended to be good Samaritans. Then they went through the gold-seekers' belongings and robbed them. Smith and his thugs intercepted prospectors who'd struck it rich in the Yukon when they were on the return trip. They were stripped of their hard-earned gold in crooked card games. Some were held up at gunpoint and robbed of everything."

"Was this crook Soapy ever arrested?" Marty asked.

"No. But a man named Frank Reid finally brought him down. Reid was a real hero. He and Soapy had an old-fashioned shootout on the town dock. Both men were mortally wounded and later died. They are buried next to each other in the Skagway cemetery."

"You tell fascinating stories, Albert," Max said.

"Good luck in your series with the Ottawa Silver Seven."

"Don't wish him too much luck, boys," McGee said, rising from the table and reaching to shake Albert by the hand. "Just kidding, young fellow," he said. "I wish you good luck too. Now you'd better get some sleep. You look exhausted."

CHAPTER 12

A MEMORABLE SERIES BEGINS

Dey's Arena was packed to capacity for the first game of the series with the visitors from the Yukon. Five thousand fans jammed the corridors and the aisles as they scrambled for their seats. The standing room in the rush end saw the usual amount of pushing and jostling for position and the usual number of fists thrown in anger as fans fought each other for the best vantage points. Young boys sneaked into the arena, who knows how? They were like mice slipping through the tiniest crack. And then they climbed up to the rafters over the ice, hanging there, holding on for dear life, laughing at the threats of burly policemen below, waving their billy clubs, ordering them to come down.

"No, you come up, coppers!" they called out, brash and insolent. They used their peashooters to discourage anyone who took the side of the lawmen.

Word spread quickly through the building. Weldy

Young, a former star with Ottawa, would not appear for the visitors in game one. His trip had been delayed by a blizzard west of Winnipeg.

"Forget Weldy! Let's play hockey!" a fan bellowed.

The Governor General arrived in his coach and walked along the red carpet leading to centre ice. There, waving to the crowd, Lord Grey dropped the puck—unofficially—between the opposing centres.

The official face-off followed. After the pre-game ceremonies, while the red carpet was being rolled up, Nigel Watt, a tall, muscular player with the Nuggets, skated up to Frank McGee. They were nose to nose by the boards, directly in front of Max and Marty.

"Get ready to take a pounding tonight," the visiting player growled.

McGee stared coldly at Watt. On almost every team he faced, there was someone who wanted to beat him up, someone who was jealous of his skills, someone who wanted to stop him in his tracks. Fortunately, he hadn't met an opponent yet who could do it, although many had tried. Now someone from the far-off Klondike was about to take him on.

A few feet away, sitting at rinkside, Marty nudged Max. "What's going on?"

"Don't know. But I think Frankie is about to explode. He looks calm, doesn't he? But deep down, his temper couldn't be hotter if it was cooked on a stove."

Watt glared down at his smaller rival. "So you're the great McGee," he sneered. "A puny little guy with his hockey pants all neatly pressed. And his hair slicked back. Yer momma do that for you?" needled the much bigger Watt.

"What's your name, big fellow?" McGee asked calmly.

"Watt's my name."

"Yes, what?" asked McGee.

"Yeah, Watt. I told you already. Watt. Watt's my name."

McGee looked surprised. "Oh, What What. Odd name—What What," said Frankie. "First and last name the same?"

"No, it's Nigel . . . Nigel . . . Watt . . . Watt. I mean Nigel Watt," Watt shouted in frustration.

Frankie smiled. "I get it. Nigel Nigel What What. Do all you Dawson boys have double names?"

"You're . . . you're . . . a sick man, McGee," said Watt, seething.

McGee threw a hand to one ear. "What? What was that, What What?"

"Dern you, McGee! Yer poking fun at me," Watt exploded, "You wait. I'll show you what's what before this game is over."

"Fine with me," said McGee calmly. "I'll watch out for you, Mr. What. Say, are you related to Walter What, the watchmaker? Or Willy What, the night watchman? Walter What owns a waterproof watch. Willy What has a watchdog."

"Why, you . . ." Nigel Watt spluttered.

"Watch it, What," McGee cautioned. "Tell you what. Don't get worked up like a whale out of water. Why not sit back and watch me walk right through you fellows?"

McGee turned to wink at Max and Marty. But they had fallen back in their seats, laughing uproariously.

When McGee turned his head, Nigel Watt took a wild swing at him. But Frankie stepped nimbly aside.

The referee, Mr. Smeaton, moved in and pushed the players apart.

"C'mon, you two. Game hasn't even started yet."

"You want a thrashing, I'll give you one," Watt threatened. "You watch yer back, McGee."

Again McGee cupped a hand to his ear. "You want to wash my back, Mr. What What? How kind of you. But I seldom get that friendly with my opponents."

Frankie smiled and skated away.

While Max and Marty were wiping tears of laughter from their eyes, Nigel Watt took his stick and smashed it against the boards, splintering it in a dozen places.

"That'll teach you," shouted Marty. "Don't mess with McGee, Mr. What What."

Nigel Watt gave Marty a murderous look. "Fresh young punks," he growled as he skated away to get a second stick.

"Did you hear that?" Marty asked.

Max put a hand to one ear. "What?"

Marty dug an elbow into his brother's ribs.

McGee was still smiling when he moved in for the opening face-off. The puck was dropped, bounced away, and Frankie made a beeline for it. He corralled it and darted into the Dawson City zone, nailing Watt with an elbow to the nose in passing that staggered the burly, slow-moving winger.

McGee whistled a shot at Forrest, then another and a third. Forrest stopped them all. McGee ripped a fourth shot off Forrest's goal stick and the deflected puck sailed into the crowd. A fan snared it and placed it in his pocket.

"Throw it back!" The fans around him shouted. "Throw it back!"

"No, I'm keeping it. For a souvenir."

"There's only one puck. Throw it back!"

"They'll find another," the fan declared.

Officials scurried into the Ottawa dressing room in search of a second puck. They had never seen a fan pocket the puck before and refuse to give it back.

"So that's how that tradition began," Max said to Marty.

During the delay, young Forrest left his goal and skated out to where Nigel Watt was standing.

"I don't think it's wise to rile McGee, Nigel," he suggested softly. "They say he's a terror when he gets angry."

"Mind yer own business, buster. Get back in goal. I'll take care of McGee. You'll see."

Max and Marty noted that Albert Forrest was limping slightly when he returned to the goal.

Albert kept the Nuggets in the game with some dazzling saves. He was particularly effective against McGee, stopping him on three breakaways. But on the fourth, McGee knocked Watt on his backside with a solid bodycheck, and then left Forrest spinning after a nifty deke that he finished off by flipping the puck into the net.

"Did you see that, Marty? Frankie deked him. What a move!"

"Albert's trying his best but he must have faced fifty shots already," Marty observed. "He's exhausted."

"And his defensemen are backing right in on him. He can't see half the Ottawa shots," Max said. "Poor Albert."

"Nigel Watt is no help," observed Marty. "He's still so mad at Frankie that he's out of position most of the time."

Forrest and his mates began to wilt in the second half. Nigel Watt, unable to stop McGee, took his anger out on tiny Harry Smith, racing forty feet across the ice to crack him over the head with his stick.

"That was so blatant," murmured Max in disgust. "Such a selfish, foolish act. He really hurt his team with that attack on Smith."

Referee Smeaton sent Watt to the box for fifteen minutes.

"Albert's in for it now," predicted Marty.

Ottawa showed no mercy and won the game 9–2. By then many of the spectators had left for home, disappointed. They had come to see a spectacle and had been witness to a slaughter.

Max and Marty had arranged to meet Albert after the game in the lobby of the Russell Hotel. They sat in overstuffed chairs and discussed the debacle.

"They gave us a bad licking, all right," Albert said. "But what a thrill it was to take part in a Stanley Cup game before all those people. I was a little nervous at first but after I stopped McGee a couple of times I settled down."

Marty said, "I talked with Coach Green after the game, Albert. He said you were the best of the visitors by far. Both the Montreal Gazette and the Ottawa Citizen are planning to do features about you."

"I hope the reporters will remind everyone that your team was exhausted after such a long journey," Max said. "And that you were playing the world champions short-handed for a long stretch."

"Thanks to a stupid penalty," added Marty. "Don't worry, Albert. You'll be a whole lot better in the second game."

A man passing behind Albert's chair overheard Marty's remark and stopped. The man's nose was beet red, as if he'd just walked into a post.

"He'd better be a whole lot better in game two," the man said gruffly. "You can't give up nine goals in a game and hope to win the Cup. Albert, I told you before, you're too young to be playing high calibre hockey. You let us down tonight."

Max bolted from his chair. "You're Nigel Watt, aren't you?"

"That's right, kid."

"Mr. Watt, I'm shocked you'd pin the blame on Albert for the loss tonight. It wasn't his fault. He played a great game. Especially when you were in the penalty box."

"A cheap penalty," Watt whined. "From that homer Smeaton."

"But I saw you cough up the puck more than once, Mr. Watt. And you let Frank McGee sift around you to score a goal."

"So what? By then the game was lost. I started saving myself for the second match."

"So you quit? You left your goaltender to do all the work."

"Didn't quit," Watt growled. "I said I was saving myself."

"Frank McGee never quits," Marty said. "Frank McGee always supports his goalie. He never blames him."

"Don't talk to me about McGee," Watt said, putting

a hand to his misshapen nose. "The so-and-so belted me with an elbow when I wasn't looking. It was a cheap shot. He's sneaky. And over-rated. He didn't look so hot tonight. He only scored one goal. On a shot Albert should have handled."

"There you go," Marty said. "Blaming your teammate."

Max smiled and said, "Frank McGee is a good friend of ours, Mr. Watt. I'll be happy to tell him you think he's over-rated."

"Tell him anything you want," Nigel Watt mumbled. He scowled at Max and Marty. "Why am I wasting my time talking hockey with a couple of squirts who know nothing about the game?" He began to stalk off. "I'm going to bed."

Max couldn't resist. He cupped his ear. "What?"

Marty stifled a laugh. "Goodnight, old beet nose," he muttered. But Watt was gone.

"Some teammate," Marty snorted. He said to Albert, "What a lousy attitude. I hope the others aren't like him."

"One or two of the others don't seem to care much about playing for the Cup," Albert sighed. "They're only here because a rich miner sponsored our trip. They won't be going back to the Yukon."

"So they joined the Nuggets just to get a cheap trip back East?" Marty asked.

"That's about it," Albert said.

"But you'll be going back, Albert."

"Sure will. I love the Yukon. The mountains, the woods, the rivers. There's no place like it." He glanced at the huge clock in the lobby. "Say, I'd better turn in," he said. He had trouble rising from his chair and he limped when he tried to walk. Max noted some blood on one of his socks.

"Albert, are you badly hurt?" Max asked, alarmed. He took the young goaltender by the arm. "What happened?"

"I pulled a muscle in my leg when McGee put that move on me. I've never seen a move like that."

"We call it a deke," Marty said, smiling at Max.

"Then Rat Westwick slashed me across the ankle late in the game. It's not a deep cut but it hurts."

"Perhaps you should see a doctor," Max suggested.

"No, no doctor. He might order me not to play tomorrow night. I didn't travel four thousand miles to play for the Stanley Cup only to watch from the sidelines. People might call me a quitter."

He smiled. "Besides, I'm the only goalie on the team. Good night, boys."

CHAPTER 13
MCGEE'S FABULOUS RECORD

Two nights later, another immense crowd turned out for game two of the Dawson City versus Ottawa series. Perhaps they had a premonition that something unique would occur, that possibly some records would be broken. History made.

There was a smattering of applause for Albert Forrest as he took his place in the Nuggets' net. He had rapidly won the hearts of the Ottawa faithful for his gritty performance in the opening game.

Everyone could see he was limping. Everyone knew he was in for a hard night's work—with very little chance of reward at the end of it.

Before the opening face-off Nigel Watt glared menacingly at McGee. But from a distance.

McGee skated up to him. "I hear you've been saying nice things about me, Watt. Like I'm a cream-puff. And over-rated."

"So those mouthy Mitchell kids have been spouting

off," said Watt. "You are over-rated, McGee. One puny goal in the first game. Against a kid still wet behind the ears. Yer a big phony, McGee."

Frankie smiled. "What?" he asked.

"Now don't start that, McGee!" Watt exploded. His nose turned red as a rose. He slammed his stick on the ice.

"Tut, tut," said referee Smeaton. "Are you ready to play hockey, Watt? Or would you rather entertain the crowd with a temper tantrum?"

The referee turned serious. "Let's play hockey!" he barked.

Just as he had done in game one, Frank McGee took command early in the game, testing Forrest with hard shots from long range, scoring on two of them.

On one patented McGee rush, Nigel Watt skated awkwardly at the Ottawa ace and attempted to lace him across the face with stick and gloves. But McGee ducked and came up with a shoulder check that rocked Watt. The collision took place near the boards and, to his amazement, Watt sailed right into the Governor General's box. In doing so, he knocked Lord Grey's tall hat from his head and would have fallen into Lady Marlene's lap if she hadn't leaped aside. She took a breath, wrinkled her nose and said, "Ugh."

"Sorry, your Highness," Watt sputtered. "I mean,

your General. No, I mean your Lord. Oh, never mind what I mean."

He scrambled out of the box and tumbled in among the spectators.

Several young men promptly sat on him and when he tried to get up, spitting and howling, they pushed him back down. One ruffled his hair. Another rubbed a coarse glove across his face. A third yanked on his jersey, tearing it at the shoulder. Finally, they picked him up bodily and tossed him back on the ice.

"Did you see that?" Watt bellowed at the referee before staggering to his feet. "Throw those hoodlums out of the rink! They should be arrested!"

"What hoodlums?" answered referee Smeaton innocently. "I didn't see nothin'. Now play hockey before I give you a penalty for leaving the ice without permission."

The next minute and a half belonged to McGee. He scored three times on young Forrest in a record time of ninety seconds. The Ottawa players noticed that Forrest had trouble moving quickly from side to side on his gimpy leg and they took advantage of the handicap. Westwick and Pulford scored three goals each and Smith added another. At the half, Ottawa was leading 10–0.

When he heard the bell, Albert Forrest skated wearily to the side of the rink where he huddled with his dejected teammates. The players wiped their sweaty brows with a single towel and gulped water from a tin cup they dipped in a bucket.

Nigel Watt stepped in front of Albert Forrest and lectured him in front of everybody.

"You couldn't stop a soccer ball," he began. "If we had any kind of goaltending we'd be winning this series."

"That's bull and you know it," Albert countered. His dander was up. He was only seventeen but he wasn't going to be bullied by Watt. "We're facing one of the greatest teams ever assembled. Most of us are trying hard. But you, Nigel, are a whiner and a quitter. You should never have taunted McGee and made him furious with us. I told you that. But you don't listen."

"You expect me to listen to a teenager?" Watt snarled. "A kid as soft and fresh as a cream pie? Forget it, pal."

"Wait a minute, Nigel," one of the Dawson players said angrily. "Albert's right. You're a disgrace as a player. We'd all be a lot happier if you'd just keep your big mouth shut."

Fuming, Watt threw his stick and gloves on the ice and stormed off to the dressing room. "Get someone else to play right wing," he shouted over his shoulder. "I'm through with hockey."

The Dawson City players were stunned. They all

knew Watt had a nasty streak. He wasn't a good team player, but they never expected him to quit in the middle of a game. A Stanley Cup game!

Forrest, the shy teenager, decided someone had to take charge. A lack of leadership had been a problem with the Nuggets from the beginning. He would have to provide some.

"Watt is gone and we have no replacement for him," he said to his mates. "But we could recruit a player sitting at rinkside to take his place. His name is Max Mitchell and he's a fine player. Frank McGee told me as much."

"Sounds good, Albert. Better than asking Ottawa to drop a player to even the sides. We need all the bodies we can muster."

Forrest motioned for Max to come over and join the discussion. "Throw on your skates, Max. You're taking over for Nigel Watt. Here's his stick and gloves."

"But Albert—"

"No buts, Max," Albert's voice had changed. It was more mature, manlier. "Listen! You said you always wanted to play in a Stanley Cup game. This may be your only chance. Now go get your skates on. Hurry!"

Max didn't argue. He was back in minutes, his skates firmly fastened, holding Nigel Watt's stick and wearing Watt's gloves.

The second half began and people noticed an immediate difference in the play of the Yukoners. They played with gusto, slamming into the faster Ottawa players at every opportunity, slowing them down, making them realize they were in a real hockey battle. They'd have to work hard for every goal.

McGee skated close to Max and said, "Glad to see you out here, pal. You've given Dawson a lift. I love it when an opponent battles back—no matter what the score."

"Frankie, I can't believe this is happening," Max said.

"Enjoy it, kid. You're playing against the best. You'll never forget this night. To make sure, on my next rush," he warned Max with a wink, "I'm going to skate around you for a goal."

"Oh, no, you're not," Max declared emphatically. "Try it and I'll knock you into the third row."

But no matter how hard Max tried, no matter how often he threw himself in McGee's path, the Ottawa star was unstoppable. It was one of those rare nights when every time he touched the puck it wound up in the Dawson net.

McGee was in superb condition and no player in the world could skate with him. He enjoyed a stretch when he scored four goals in two minutes and twenty seconds. He scored eight consecutive goals—another record—and finished his night's work with fourteen. The final score was Ottawa 23, Dawson 2.

Max and the rest of the Dawson City boys were exhausted from trying to check McGee into the ice. Max set up both the Dawson goals with some slick passing and playmaking. At the final bell, McGee was the first to reach Albert Forrest and pump his hand.

"Sorry if I embarrassed you, Albert," he said. "Nigel Watt made me so angry I wanted to score thirty goals. I wasn't trying to show you up."

"I understand, Frankie," Albert said, smiling and slapping McGee on the back. "You're the greatest player I've ever seen. You set records tonight that will last a lifetime. The way I look at it, I helped you set them. That's something. Isn't it, Frankie?"

McGee threw his arms around Albert and gave him a hug. "You're a great competitor and a wonderful goalie, Albert." The crowd howled its approval.

Then McGee skated over to Max.

"Great game, Max. Or should I say half a game. Now you know the thrill of competing for the Stanley Cup. For every winner, there's a loser. You and Albert were on the wrong end of the score this time but who knows? Maybe you'll both get a second chance someday."

"It was a remarkable experience," Max said. "And

you were phenomenal, Frank. Fans will be talking about your fourteen goals a hundred years from now. And I was on the ice when you did it. Albert seems to be taking the loss well. He's got character and a fine attitude."

"He's a fine young man. And an outstanding goalie. Forget the score. If it hadn't been for Albert, we would have pumped in twice as many goals. He made some spectacular saves."

CHAPTER 14

A GIFT FOR LADY MARLENE

Early the following morning, Max and Marty joined Albert for breakfast at the Russell Hotel. Albert and his teammates would be departing on the transcontinental train in little more than an hour.

"Is Nigel Watt going back with you?" Marty asked as he spread several lumps of brown sugar on his oatmeal.

"No. He checked out after the game last night. Told the desk clerk he was going to stay with some friends here in Ottawa. Nobody shed any tears. He showed his true colours in this series."

"Hockey has a way of bringing out a player's character—good and bad," Max said. "I feel sorry for anyone who doesn't experience the sheer joy of playing the game."

"Especially when it's for the Stanley Cup," Marty added.

"How are you feeling this morning, Albert?" Max

asked. "Now that all the excitement is over."

Albert flashed a smile. "Max, I'm sore all over. Every muscle hurts. But I'm glad I came. Playing against Frank McGee was the thrill of a lifetime."

"The morning paper credits you with an excellent performance despite . . . well . . . what happened," Marty said, pointing at the headline on the sports page. "The reporter says your teammates could have given you a lot more support. And that Nigel Watt acted deplorably."

Albert grinned. "I won't knock my teammates. All but one. They did the best they could. Hey, I got a telegram from my folks. They're still proud of me. And Dawson City is planning a parade and a banquet for the players when we get home—those that are going home."

He looked at the clock on the wall. "Gotta go, boys. Got a train to catch. It sure was a pleasure meeting you. Come and see me in Dawson City someday. We'll go prospecting for gold."

Max and Marty walked Albert across the street to the train station, where he hoisted his travel bag over his shoulder, waved them a final farewell and hopped aboard the train leaving for Vancouver.

"We're going to miss Albert," Max said as the train disappeared from sight.

"I wish we could go hunting for gold in the Yukon," Marty said. "Maybe I'd discover a big mine and have someone make me a gold hockey stick—the first one in history."

"Sure," scoffed Max. "And how would you ever lift it off the ice?"

It began to snow. The brothers crossed the street and sat in the lobby of the Russell Hotel. Frank McGee had dropped them there before hurrying off to hockey practice.

Marty said, "I hope Albert strikes it rich in the Yukon. He deserves to be successful."

Max grinned. "Won't happen, brother. The gold rush is over. No more fortunes will be made. Or lost. But Albert will be a success at whatever he chooses to do. We both know that."

"You're right, Max. Now that the Dawson City series is over, do you think we should go home? Go back to Indian River?"

"Not unless you want to swim up the River of Time," Max answered. "The ice broke up last week. We'll have to stay for another hockey season. Besides, I want to see how long the Silver Seven can hold onto the Stanley Cup."

"But our folks will be worried. Our friends . . ."

"Marty, nobody knows we're gone. Nobody knows we're here in Ottawa having the time of our lives."

"You're having the time of your life. You played in a Stanley Cup game. I didn't. And now you're going sledding and skating and snowshoeing with Lady Marlene. Pretty soon you'll never want to go home. You know what I think? I think you're falling in love."

Max grinned. He shook Marty by one shoulder. "What do you know about love, little brother? Are you worried that I'll decide to stay here in Ottawa and start courting her? Maybe even marry her someday?"

"Yeah, I was thinking . . ."

"Forget about it, Marty. Soon we'll have to go back to Indian River. That's where we belong. And Marlene belongs at Government House. At least for now." Max sighed and looked off in the distance.

"In a few months, when we're back home, Lord Grey will be replaced as Governor General and Lady Marlene will return with her family to England. She has no choice in the matter. Her family will arrange for her to meet a Lord or a Viscount or some rich guy with a fancy title when she's ready for marriage. Her life is all mapped out for her."

"She might marry a Duke, Max," said Marty. "Remember, we had a dog named Duke once. Used to slobber all over Mom's carpet."

Max winced at the thought of Marlene marrying a slobbering Duke.

"Marlene and I have become great friends, Marty," Max said softly. "But the sad part of our trip here—

at least for me—is that soon I'll never see her again. But in some strange way, I know we'll never forget each other. We'll always remember the good times we've enjoyed here in Ottawa."

Max fished in his pocket and pulled out a small package, tied with a red ribbon.

"What's that?" Marty asked.

"A small gift for Marlene."

"But what is it?"

"A hockey puck. From the final game against Dawson City."

"A hockey puck? For Marlene? Geez, that's not much of a gift."

"I know it's not much. Three inches of vulcanized rubber. But she said she wanted a souvenir of hockey, a puck that she could take back to England when she goes. She said every time she looks at it, she'll remember attending the games here and one in particular—the one I played in. Now what do you think?"

"Max, I think a hockey puck is the best gift you could give her. The very best."

CHAPTER 15
A FINAL CONFRONTATION
FOR THE CUP

It appeared that the Stanley Cup would slip out of the hands of the Ottawa Silver Seven during the 1906 hockey season. But even if it did, the team had fashioned a remarkable record over the past three seasons—seventeen wins, two defeats and two tie games.

One winter morning, Marty Mitchell thrust the Ottawa Citizen in front of Max and said, "Look! Last night in a game at Montreal, a goalie scored a goal. It says Fred Brophy of Montreal skated down the ice and shot the puck into the opposing team's net."

"I've never heard of that before," Max said. "Hockey is full of surprises, isn't it?"

"Especially this season. I'm surprised the Ottawa club agreed to meet a challenge from Queen's University," Marty stated. "Frankie said the college boys would be as weak as Dawson City and he was right. Ottawa swamped Queens in the two games 16–7 and 12–7.

"Then they demolished Smiths Falls, the next challengers, by scores of 6–5 and 8–2. Frankie scored nine goals in those games. You know he's averaging three goals a game in Cup games. Nobody's come close to that."

"Even so," Max said, "Ottawa and the Montreal Wanderers finished in a tie for the league title—each with 9–1 records. They're going to meet in a two-game, total goal series beginning tomorrow night in Montreal. Frankie wants us to go to Montreal with the team on the morning train—after he gets a cast on his wrist."

Marty looked up from the paper. "What's the matter with his wrist?"

"Didn't you hear? He almost broke it in the game against Smiths Falls. Someone slashed him. It's so painful he can barely move his right hand."

"Then Ottawa's chances aren't good. In fact, they're doomed."

Max said, "There's another problem the public doesn't know about. The team held a vote in the dressing room the other night about who would replace Harvey Pulford as captain. Most of the players wanted Frankie. But one or two insisted on Rat Westwick. A terrible argument broke out. Frankie had left before it started. But you know what happens when there's dissension on a team. Everything goes downhill. It doesn't look good."

Marty sighed. "Oh, well. If the Silver Seven can hang in and win the next two games, the season will be over. And they'll still be Cup champs. They'll go down in history as a hockey dynasty."

"Wishful thinking, Marty. With Frankie badly injured and Eldon Hague, the new goaltender, giving up too many goals, the team is weaker than it's ever been."

Marty snorted. "Hague is a sieve. I could play better than him. If the Ottawa management had signed Albert Forrest when he was here, they'd have no problems in goal. None at all."

The following night, a nervous Eldon Hague led the Ottawa team onto the ice of the huge arena in Montreal. The partisan Montreal fans booed him mercilessly, just as they booed all visiting goaltenders. But the chilly reception appeared to startle the rookie goaltender. His hands began to tremble and a look of panic crossed his face. This was the most pressure he'd ever faced in hockey and he wondered if he was up to it.

The next hour provided the answer: he wasn't.

Supported by a constant roar of encouragement, the Montrealers, paced by a brilliant new player named Lester Patrick, outskated, outscored, and manhandled the despised visitors from the nation's capital. They feasted on the porous goaltending of Eldon Hague, who was jeered after every goal.

Frank McGee, sporting a white cast on his wrist, became a favourite target for the confident Wanderers. They hacked and slashed at his cast, hoping to break enough small bones to put McGee on the sidelines.

"That's mean and nasty of them," Marty said angrily. "They're rotten sports to try and maim McGee."

Max smiled. "Frank has them fooled. He's a pretty smart player."

"What do you mean? They're trying to kill him."

"Don't tell anyone, Marty. But Frankie had the team doctor put the cast on his good wrist. That's the one the Wanderers keep slashing. And they've taken three penalties for it already."

Despite having a man advantage for several minutes, the Silver Seven were no match for the Wanderers in the opener of the series—total goals to count. They lost by 9–1.

The Wanderers' Lester Patrick outshone every other player on the ice. He had replaced Punch Pounder on the Montreal roster after Pounder was suspended for a year for assaulting a referee.

"Patrick was sensational," Marty groaned. "Even Frankie had trouble defending against him."

"Looks like he'll be around for a long time," agreed Max. "Still, it was weak goaltending that cost Frankie's team the game."

Back in Ottawa, the stage was set for the second game. Montreal's 9–1 lead in goals was a huge advantage. Insurmountable, almost everyone agreed. It almost certainly meant the end of the incredible winning record of the Ottawa hockey club.

Petey Green, the Ottawa coach, dared not put Eldon Hague back in goal. The local sportswriters had roasted Hague. He was so badly shaken by the loss in Montreal that he had threatened to throw himself off the bridge into the Ottawa River. His mother told a reporter, "I won't let my Eldon play another game. Those greedy Montrealers treated him shamefully, piling up the score like they did. I fear for Eldon's health. He is close to a breakdown. I hope he will play croquet from now on."

Frank McGee said, "I would love to see our team sign Albert Forrest to replace Eldon, but that's impossible. He could never get back to Ottawa in time. My next choice would be young Percy LeSueur of Smiths Falls. He's going to become famous some-day for his netminding."

Smiths Falls was only an hour's train ride away and LeSueur was rushed into uniform prior to the second Stanley Cup match at Dey's Arena.

"I'll keep the puck out at my end," the tall, shy farm boy confidently told his new teammates. "It's up to you fellows to fill the net at the other end."

These words from the newcomer gave the Ottawa players new-found life and renewed faith in themselves. They were still the champions, after all, and they would not give up the Stanley Cup without battling to the final bell. The thousands of supportive fans who had loyally backed their efforts over the years deserved no less.

A rumour swept through Ottawa that Frank McGee, the greatest player in Ottawa's rich hockey history, the man who averaged three goals per game in Cup play, would announce his retirement after the game, well shy of his 30th birthday.

"If the rumour is true, what a sad day tomorrow's going to be," Max said to Marty. "There'll never be another Frank McGee."

"He's in great condition," Marty said. "I'll bet he plays another ten years. Or even twenty. And I'll bet you another thing. He'll live to be a hundred."

Max gave his brother a strange look. A dark image had crossed his mind. "I wouldn't bet on the latter," he said quietly.

CHAPTER 16

MCGEE'S LAST CHANCE

When the Silver Seven skated onto their home ice
for game two, trailing in the series by eight goals, a
fan bellowed at his idol Frank McGee. "Say it ain't
so, Frankie! Don't quit! Don't ever leave us!"

The fans applauded the man's plea and when
McGee took a whirl around the arena ice, the ovation he received was deafening.

"McGee! McGee! McGee!"

Frankie trembled with emotion. Tears flowed from
his good eye. He waved to his fans. Soon they would
learn that he had decided to retire at the end of the
match. Then, head down, thoughts of everything
else but winning were erased from his mind. He was
fully aware that a victory was almost impossible—
not with his team needing eight goals—just to gain
a tie.

He skated into position and prepared for the
drop of the puck. He all but ignored the Governor

General's ceremonial face-off, allowing the opposing centre to snap up the puck and present it to Lord Grey. Somehow he was able to mute the blaring renditions of the band, the yelps and howls from the raucous crowd. He smiled only once—to acknowledge the wave and the smile that Lady Marlene Grey threw in his direction. After that his features turned grim. He was determined to show the hometown fans that their team—his team—was not finished. He had scored fourteen goals in a Stanley Cup game, hadn't he? Perhaps eight or nine, against stiffer competition, was still within his reach.

He realized the Wanderers would be double-teaming him, determined to keep him off the scoresheet. What I'll do tonight, he thought, is make good passes to my linemates and not worry so much about scoring myself.

The Silver Seven came out flying and it was McGee who set the torrid pace. He and his left winger, the talented Harry Smith, owned the puck. It rattled back and forth between them and it was Smith who whacked in three fast goals. McGee's passes to Smith were perfectly timed.

"Way to go, Smitty!" McGee shouted.

"Thanks for the great passes, Frankie," Smith hollered back.

"Stop him! Stop McGee!" barked Lester Patrick, the Wanderers' star.

McGee's fierce play and his determined forecheck-ing rattled the Wanderers. They could not escape their own zone and it cost them. McGee intercepted a pass and threw the puck once again to Harry Smith. Goal!

Moments later, McGee made a dazzling rink-length rush and banged in another Ottawa goal. Before the cheering died down, he did it again, fin-ishing off his rush with a deke that left the Montreal goalie sprawling on his backside.

The Wanderers' lead had been whittled to two.

The fans were in an uproar. The din from the arena carried through the cold winter air and could be heard a mile away.

Montrealers in the rink were silent. They were in shock, in despair. Hundreds had travelled by train to the big game. They had counted on a sweet victory celebration afterward and a prolonged party atmos-phere aboard the train that would take them home.

But McGee was en route to shattering their hopes and their plans. A 9–1 Wanderers lead had quickly shrunk, like woollen underwear in a tub of hot water. Montreal 9. Ottawa 7.

For the visiting fans, it was a calamity. Even the great Lester Patrick looked like a pond hockey player next to McGee. As for Ottawa's new goalie, LeSueur, the kid was showing remarkable poise. He was unflappable. Obviously he was going to be a star puckstopper for many years to come. Time and again, he turned back the Montreal attackers, leaving them shaking their heads in frustration and disbelief. Only one puck eluded him, a high shot to the corner of the net. The visitors led by 10–7.

Lester Patrick breathed a sigh of relief.

Early in the second half, Rat Westwick scored for Ottawa and celebrated by throwing his stick high in the air. He turned to embrace a teammate, and, having forgotten the stick, was stunned when it came down on his head, cutting him for three stitches. Montreal 10, Ottawa 8.

The Silver Seven were two goals behind but were enjoying a remarkable surge in momentum, unlike anything their fans had ever witnessed in Dey's Arena.

Lester Patrick was no fool. He wisely called for a one-minute time out. Patrick, a master of motivation, gathered his mates around him and gave them an eloquent pep talk. When his talk lasted more than a minute, he pretended he didn't hear referee Smeaton's demand that play continue. The crowd booed Patrick to the rafters but he ignored the jeers and catcalls. By the time play resumed, his men were rested.

"Come on, fellows," he pleaded. "This is your big chance to win the Cup. It may be your only chance. Stop McGee any way you can. Lose this game and people will laugh at you. The humiliation will be unbearable."

"Play hockey, Lester!" Smeaton shouted in anger. "I warned you. I'm facing the puck with or without you."

The crowd was furious with Patrick but their boos turned to cheers when referee Smeaton threw the puck into the corner of the rink. "Go chase it!" he told the surprised players.

"Hey, that's not fair!" complained Patrick. "We weren't ready." But there was no time for further argument. He and his mates scrambled after it.

Heeding Patrick's words, the Wanderers checked furiously, constantly sneaking glances at the clock. Three minutes to play! In three minutes they'd win the Cup. In three minutes the wild celebration would begin. They were determined to avoid the humiliation Patrick had warned them about.

McGee's wrist came under further attack. He was slashed and held and tripped. No penalties.

"I'm not calling penalties this late in the game," the referee barked, setting a trend that would continue in playoff hockey for decades.

McGee was battered and bruised but somehow willed his weary legs to make two final rushes. They were brilliantly executed and each one paid off in a goal. One was a classic "deke," the other a variation of "Uncle Jake's move." On the latter, he faked a move behind the net and when the Wanderer goalie moved quickly to the other post. McGee whirled around the surprised goal judge, came out the way he'd started in, and slipped the puck into the cage.

The explosion of sound that greeted his series-tying goal was equal to fifty thunderstorms. Fans threw hats and foot rubbers and their newly printed programs—with advertising—onto the ice. Five thousand voices shrieked "McGee! McGee! McGee!"

Max and Marty had never witnessed such excitement. They jumped up and hugged each other and added their voices to the mighty roar.

"I wouldn't have missed this for the world," Max shouted over the din. "What a hockey game!"

"What a hero Frankie is," Marty shouted back. "If he scores one more goal, Ottawa will hold the Cup. I'll bet you Frankie does it."

"I'm with you," Max countered. "I'd never bet against Frankie."

Fans could almost reach out and feel the tension in the arena before play resumed. Two minutes on the clock and McGee was on fire. Surely the Silver Seven would hold the Cup for another year. Another goal would do it.

"One more goal! One more goal!" shrieked the Ottawa fans.

But on the ice, while a dozen sweepers were vigorously cleaning the surface of debris, Lester Patrick could be seen exhorting his players once again.

"We are not beaten," he cried. "We are tied. We will not let Ottawa win. We are their equal and there is still time left. We will not lose this game!"

Play commenced and Patrick soon showed his actions were as good as his chatter. He started a rush down the right wing and with a series of brilliant moves, found an opening to the net. He dashed through it. He pulled LeSueur to one side and slipped the puck through his legs.

There was a collective gasp from the Ottawa fans. It was as if every one of them had been hit in the stomach with a broomstick. Or a knife. It seemed impossible that Montreal would score, when all of the play, all of the scoring chances, had been Ottawa's.

But it was true. The arena was as silent as a country cemetery, as sombre and cheerless as a haunted house.

Then, from one of the back rows, an urgent voice called out, "There's still time, Ottawa! There's still time! You can do it, Frankie!"

But there was only time enough left if Ottawa could snare the puck and send McGee off on one final dazzling, desperate rush. And with mere seconds left to play, the Wanderers controlled the rubber.

It was Patrick who refused to give it up, who

whirled and darted and fled his attackers. It was Patrick who spun away from McGee's final, frantic check. And it was Patrick who slipped through an opening and whipped a hard shot at Lesueur. The puck skimmed along the ice, struck the goal post and bounced over the black line into the net. Just as the bell clanged to end the game. Montreal 12, Ottawa 10.

In despair, young LeSueur cracked his stick on the ice.

"No, no, no!" he wailed. "I should have had it."

The Ottawa players stood in shock, unable to believe their fate. They were crestfallen, dazed, sick with disappointment. The new champions pranced around the ice in glee, in celebration of a momentous victory. The Wanderers were Stanley Cup champions. The glorious era of hockey supremacy in Ottawa was over.

And the fabulous career of One-Eyed Frank McGee had also come to an end. Tearfully, he told his mates, "I'm finished, men. Through with hockey. You'll have to carry on without me." They gathered around him, wiping their eyes, consoling him, patting him on the back.

Lester Patrick led his Wanderers to the gathering and gently pushed their way to the core. Lester and two of his mates hoisted McGee up and onto broad shoulders. They paraded him around the rink, showing the Ottawa fans they recognized his greatness, showing respect and sportsmanship, triggering another explosion of applause. When they set him down, each one shook his hand. Some had him autograph their sticks.

McGee acknowledged the standing ovation by waving in all directions. He found it hard to speak. But always the sportsman, he grasped the hand of silver-haired Lester Patrick.

"You killed us with those final two goals, Lester. You're a real champion. Congratulations."

"Thank you, Frank," Lester said, pumping McGee's hand. "You scared us half to death tonight. You almost pulled off the greatest comeback in hockey history. My boys said chasing after you was like chasing after a ghost. Please tell me you're not going to retire."

Frank's words fought their way past a huge lump in his throat. "I think it's time," he sighed. "Hockey has given me a wonderful life. But it's not the only thing in life. Here in Ottawa I've met a lot of politicians over the years. Perhaps I can contribute as much or more to my country than some of them."

"You can do better than most of them," Lester Patrick assured him. "Much better. You're a born leader, Frankie. You can even be Prime Minister one day. Rest assured, we're all behind you. Good luck, my friend."

Frank McGee skated slowly across the ice, as if reluctant to leave. The fans remained standing. They accorded him a final tribute, a thunderous ovation. He wished the moment would never end. As he approached the gate, he pulled off a glove and tossed it high into the crowd. A young boy snatched it out of mid air. The other glove followed. Another young fan made the catch and stuffed the glove inside his coat.

McGee waved to his parents and family members, sitting several rows back from the ice. Then he turned and skated to the Governor General's box. He leaned over and placed his hockey stick, a stick that had produced so many goals over the season, into the hands of Lady Marlene.

She rose from her seat, leaned over the rail and gave McGee a spontaneous hug and a kiss. The spectators roared in approval.

"Thank you, Frank McGee," she whispered. "I'll never forget you. Never!"

She turned and cried into her mother's shoulder, into the lace handkerchief she held in one hand.

With a final wave to the crowd, flashing his familiar engaging smile, Frank McGee reached the open gate. He paused for a moment, took a breath, and stepped through. He was gone from sight.

Never again would McGee's flashing blades light up Dey's Arena; never again would he be the peerless leader of the Silver Seven; never again would he be the sensation of hockey, his name synonymous with excellence on ice, the darling of the crowd, the player nobody could stop.

At rinkside, Max and Marty were all weepy-eyed.

"I really thought Ottawa would hang onto the Cup," Marty said. "I was sure Frankie would come through one more time."

"I wish he had," stated Max. "He came so close. But champions can't stay on top forever. Dynasties come and go in sports and now Ottawa's long reign has ended. As Frankie would say, 'That's hockey.'"

Marty pulled a handkerchief from his pocket and blew his nose. "There'll be buckets of tears shed in the city tonight," he said, "while all those Montrealers in town will be drinking champagne from the Cup."

Max wiped his eyes one more time and rose from his seat. "Come on. We'll go see Frankie one last time. And say goodbye to the rest of the team."

"Let's go," Marty said. "I want to thank them for taking our suggestions seriously. And I want to tell Frankie he's the greatest athlete I've ever met. And the greatest person."

Max began to smile. He nudged his brother. "Hasn't this been a wonderful adventure for us, Marty? Aren't you glad you came?"

"I sure am. But I'll be happy to get home, too."

"We'll be off in the morning, Marty. We can't stay any longer. It's time to head back up the River of Time."

"If I fall in on the way back, will you pull me out?" Marty asked impishly. "Or do you just save damsels in distress? Like Lady Marlene?"

"You still got the fifty cents in your pocket for ice cream cones?"

"Yep."

"Then I'll be sure to haul you out."

CHAPTER 17

HOME AGAIN

Max opened his eyes, blinked several times and gradually woke up. He looked over and saw Marty about to get up. His brother was smiling.

"I feel great, really great," Marty exclaimed, stretching his arms over his head. "Did you have the same dream I had? You did, didn't you? I can tell. Wasn't it awesome?"

Max stood up and rubbed his eyes. "It was awesome. Even better than awesome. I feel so . . . so full of energy and happiness. Like I've just experienced the adventure of a lifetime. Hey, let's go see the Chief," he suggested.

Outside the longhouse the boys found Chief Echo sitting on a log. He was cleaning a fat trout he'd caught.

"You're back!" Chief Echo exclaimed. "Sit down, sit down." He shifted along the log, making room. "Look at the fish I caught! Tell me, did you have a pleasant dream? Did you go down the River of Time? Did you skate with Frank McGee? Did you . . ."

"Hold on, Chief Echo," Max answered, laughing. "We did all of those things and more. It was amazing."

"Tell me all about it. I can't wait to hear."

Vivid memories of Ottawa flashed through Max's mind; the deep snow, the hockey games, the one-horse sleigh, the violet eyes of Lady Marlene. He told Chief Echo the full story, speaking so quickly that Marty grasped him by the arm, halting the flow of words.

"My brother could talk the teeth out of a saw," Marty said. "Let me tell the rest of the story."

Marty talked about the Dawson City series and how Max played as a "ringer," substituting for Nigel Watt.

"Max even beat the Great Frank McGee in a skating race at Government House. And I got to play against him in a practice at Dey's Arena. I was terrific, Chief. I stopped Frankie every time."

"He did, Chief Echo," Max confirmed, but with a wink. "Every time."

"And you followed One-Eyed Frank McGee's career until it was over?" Chief Echo asked, wanting to hear more.

"Just his hockey career, sir. He starred in football as well. And he was a golfer and curler. They called him the greatest athlete and sportsman in Ottawa's history. We didn't get to see him perform much in those other sports. We had to come back. It was time."

"I just thought of something," Marty said, snapping his fingers. "This is 1936, right? Maybe Frankie's still alive. Maybe we could go to Ottawa and meet him sometime soon. In real life. He'd be in his fifties by now."

Max had some reservations. "Maybe we could. But what if he didn't know who we were, even though we were best friends for a short time—in our dreams, at least?"

Max stood up.

"Max," Marty said, "there's something sticking out of your back pocket. You never carry anything in that pocket."

Max reached behind him and fished a newspaper out of his pocket. He stared at it in wonder.

"That's really odd," he said. "It's a copy of the Ottawa Citizen, dated September 25, 1916. It's old and yellow. I don't know how it found its way to my pocket. I can't explain it."

"Hmm," murmured Chief Echo. "Perhaps the Little People . . ."

Max read the headline across the top of the front page and blanched.

"No!" he groaned.

"Read it to me," Marty asked. "Read it!"

Max sat down and read aloud the story under the headline.

One of Ottawa's favourite sons, Lieut. Frank McGee, has been killed in action in France. He was killed during the great offensive on the Somme. The late Lieut. McGee was a famous hockey player during his earlier years with the Ottawa Silver Seven. He is survived by his parents, Mr. and Mrs. John McGee, brothers Darcy McGee, W.R. McGee (now in France), Jim McGee and sisters Lillian and Mary McGee. Another brother, Capt. Charles McGee was killed in France almost one year ago.

"Geez, the McGee family lost two sons in the Great War," Marty noted.

Max read on.

None of Ottawa's losses in the Great War will be regretted more than the loss of Frank McGee. He endeared himself to the sporting public as a centreman and member of the Stanley Cup champions at the height of their fame. He was universally regarded as the most brilliant and effective player ever to fill that position. Remarkably, he played most of his career with sight in only one eye and it is said he enlisted in the army by having a friend take the eye test for him.

A military spokesman told this newspaper, "Just as in his athletic career, McGee was always to be found in the thickest of the fray. He knew no fear nor shunned any danger in performance of his duty. When wounded recently, he had the option of returning to a position of safety but refused to do so, stating he wanted to be with his regiment until the job was accomplished.

Max stopped reading. He brushed away a tear and took a deep breath. He handed the paper to Marty and cupped his chin in his hands.

"There's more here," Marty said quietly. "It's written by a sports editor named Grant—Billy Grant. Should I read it?"

"Sure," Max said sadly.

When I moved to Ottawa from the West a few years ago, someone urged me to see a hockey game. They escorted me into this cold rink and I wondered how people could stand the freeze.

I heard a strange clatter of skates as the Ottawa players scrambled down from their dressing room. The voices in the rink began to hum. Then a wild roar of applause as thousands of excited voices wildly shouted, "McGee! McGee! McGee!" I drew in my breath as my companion pointed to a 130-pound, fair-haired, blue-eyed stripling who came down last. His hair was perfectly parted. His spotless white pants were creased to a knife-like edge. His boots had been polished. His skates glistened under the arc lights. And his complexion seemed as pink as a child's.

I stood spellbound.

Then someone formally introduced us and McGee

threw off a gauntlet and held out a soft but muscular hand. Then he jumped over the rail amidst another wild whoop of delight.

I saw him seize the puck at centre, skate in with the speed of a prairie cyclone and shoot—hard and accurately. I saw him backcheck, dodge here and there, flash from side to side, stickhandle his way through a knot of bigger players, slap the puck into an open corner of the net and go down in a heap as he did so. He was truly magnificent, dodging here and there, the central figure in a maze of red, white and black barber pole jerseys, followed eagerly by five thousand pairs of eyes and greeted at every turn by applause that shook the arena.

Years later, I saw him about to enter another arena, looking grim and determined on a raw November day in 1914. There was snow in the air and winter was approaching. A band played martial music as McGee and his mates swung along, untried and untrained. Many had not yet received their first lessons in the great—though costly—game they were about to play across the sea. Friends who turned out to see McGee lead his unit off, little realized that they were then waving a last farewell to the greatest hockey player of all time.

Contacted in London, former Governor General Lord Earl Grey said, "Frank McGee was the most splendid athlete I ever met. He is well remembered by my family and me from our days at Government House in Ottawa. My daughter Marlene, now the wife of Viscount Eton, named her first child Francis Michael in honour of the superb Ottawa sportsman.

Jim McGee received a letter from his brother a few days before his death. Included in the letter was a poem Frank McGee asked his brother to make public if he should be killed in uniform:

Don't grieve for me, for now I'm free!
I follow the plan God made for me.
I saw His face, I heard His call,
I took His hand and left it all . . .
I could not stay another day,
To love, to laugh, to work or play;
Tasks left undone must stay that way
And if my parting has left a void,
Then fill it with remembered joy,
A friendship shared, a laugh, a kiss,
Ah, yes, these things I, too, shall miss,
My life's been full, I've savoured much:
Good times, good friends, a loved-one's touch,
Perhaps my time seemed all too brief—
Don't shorten yours with undue grief,
Be not burdened with tears of sorrow,
Enjoy the sunshine of the morrow.

Marty's voice cracked when he read the final line. He glanced at Max and noticed more tears rolling down his brother's cheeks.

Chief Echo, fishing knife in hand, sat impassively. He was wise enough to remain silent.

"Goodbye, Frankie. We'll miss you," Max said softly.

"Hey, hey, hey," Marty said, jumping up and taking Max by the arm. "Let's go home, brother. Let's go home. Mom and Dad will be waiting. And Big Fella, too."

THE REST OF THE STORY

While some characters in The Stanley Cup Dream are fictional—like Punch Pounder, Nigel Watt and Lady Marlene—others—like Frank McGee, Lester Patrick and Percy LeSueur—were extraordinary hockey men of the era. McGee's fourteen goals in one Stanley Cup game has remained a record for over a hundred years and his 63 goals in 22 playoff games is another record not likely to be matched or shattered by any modern-day star. McGee was inducted into the Hockey Hall of Fame as one of the original twelve members in 1945.

Lester Patrick enjoyed one of the longest careers in hockey history. He began as a player in 1903–04 and continued as a coach, general manager, team owner and league organizer. His long association with the New York Rangers ended in 1947, the year he was inducted into the Hockey Hall of Fame.

Percy LeSueur's career in hockey spanned fifty years as a player, coach, sportswriter and broadcaster. He was the first manager of the Detroit Olympia— home of the Red Wings—in 1927. He became a Hockey Hall of Famer in 1961.

The Stanley Cup stories at the beginning of the book are factual. The Cup was left on a Montreal street corner. It was dropkicked into the Rideau

Canal. Chummy Hill was credited with a Stanley Cup goal in 1902—even though he scored with just half a puck. King Clancy did play every position, including goal, in a Stanley Cup match in 1923.

It's also a fact that in 1868 a crazed gunman assassinated Frank McGee's relative, Thomas D'Arcy McGee, a prominent Canadian politician.

And yes, Lord Grey did donate the Grey Cup to football.

I hope you've enjoyed this journey down the River of Time; and that you'll follow the further adventures of the Mitchell brothers in the next book in this series.